WINGS OF LOVE

Linda Windsor

A KISMET™ Romance

METEOR PUBLISHING CORPORATION
Bensalem, Pennsylvania

To my warm and wonderful family . . . thanks for the faith.

LINDA WINDSOR

Linda Windsor writes both modern and historical romances in her Salisbury home on the eastern shore of Maryland. A wife and mother of two, she manages to find enough time from running the family business with her brother to pursue her musical interests, her second love to writing, by singing and playing guitar with her husband and friends. She would love to hear from any of you who share her ageless enthusiasm for romance. You can write to Linda at P.O. Box 2597, Salisbury, MD 21801.

ONE

The visibility was magnificent. So few people could appreciate the true beauty of the Texas landscape without a panoramic bird's-eye view, and that's exactly what Kelly Benson had. Lush green hills, forested with sweet gum, cypress, ash, and oak, to mention only a few, sloped down to turquoise lakes, dotted with white sails. Geometric citrus plantations, their fields meticulously organized grids, and breathtakingly beautiful rose farms added color only mother nature could paint on such a canvas. Bluebonnets grew wild in the meadows where cattle grazed lazily on the summer day, not bothering to stir as her single-engine plane swooped low for a closer look.

There was hardly a cloud in the intense blue sky that matched the shade of the young woman's eyes as the Cessna 150 cut a lazy path, the sun reflecting off of its shiny polished sides. Upon seeing some men on equipment in a green sorghum field, she made a circle and tipped the Cessna's wings in greeting before pushing on toward Corpus Christi.

A smile spread on her tanned face, one that would have dazzled the waving farmhands below if they could have seen it. Her spirits were as high as her plane and it showed in the sparkle of her eyes, which were shaded by the curved tinted aviator's glasses she wore. Pale blonde hair cut in a stylish and easy-care wedge bounced as she tossed her head back and laughed. How shocked they would be to see that the pilot of the plane was a girl—just as shocked as the guys back at the hangar were going to be when she told them she had passed her aerobatics training.

She hadn't told them how she was going to spend her vacation from Custom Aero, where she was employed as a corporate pilot, or where she had been going every weekend for what seemed like months and months. It had taken up every spare cent she had, but the thrill was worth it. She lived for the excitement of flying. It was and had been her life and main source of income for six years. Her mastery of aerobatics, or trick flying, was just icing on the cake, although she knew even more advanced levels lay ahead for her.

The shimmering blue waters of the Gulf loomed ahead, limitless to the eastern horizon. Breaking in the distance was the skyline of Corpus Christi. Of course, Kelly would not veer north to the corporate airfield until circling beyond the staggered cluster of buildings, which appeared like a toy city below, without first taking her favorite sweep over Padre Island. The bathers at the national park looked like ants moving under and around brightly designed umbrellas in front of the pavilion. While further down the bleached white dunes, sea oats and morning glories survived heartily on unspoiled, shifting sands.

As the Cessna left the barrier island that guarded the coast and set its course for the Custom Aero airfield, Kelly turned up the volume of her transceiver to monitor the company frequency. Ahead lay the fenced-in acres of the site where customwork of almost any nature imaginable was done on aircraft of all types. Custom Aero's engineers were among the sharpest in the world and their factory was known for its excellent work. Individuals with thousands to millions to spend, or companies with specific needs patronized the multi-million dollar corporation that had grown from a small business Dan Mooney and her father, George Benson, had founded thirty years ago.

Dan Mooney had put up the money, but it was her father who was the technical brain of the team. They had been equal partners until her father died of a heart attack. Her mother, an attractive Swedish woman of forty, inherited his half of the company. The inheritance was as much an attraction as her mother's fair beauty, so it wasn't long before she remarried, a marriage that was the woman's undoing. Then, in less than five years, her new husband had robbed her of her inheritance and her pride.

Kelly had only been sixteen, but she still remembered the day Uncle Dan had bought out her mother's share of the business when she was forced to liquidate her stock in order to pay off Harold Carson's gambling debts. Kelly had driven her mother to the attorneys' office that day because, as usual, her mother was too intoxicated to operate the car. She watched for two more years as her mother destroyed herself—or what was left, after the opportunist had run off with another older widow with a hefty inheritance—with alcohol. Yet, even on her deathbed, Marta Benson had loved the handsome fortune hunter.

To this day, Kelly could not understand how her mother could have been so foolish. The young playboy had used her. He had treated her abominably. He had even propositioned eighteen-year-old Kelly, something Kelly never told her mother, just before he deserted them both. Kelly had spat in his face, venting all the pent-up anger that had festered as she watched her mother waste away.

Never would she ever be victim to a man like that, she'd vowed as she stood by her mother's graveside. Never would she expose her heart to men. They were not to be trusted, especially the good-looking ones. As she grew older, she realized that when her father and Uncle Dan had been made, the mold had been broken. No one ever measured up to their standards. And then she met Ken Hudson.

Ken was chief engineer at the plant, having worked his way up from a junior level. He was as fiercely aggressive in his field as Kelly was accused of being in hers—never satisfied until they had reached the top. Their similar interests had brought them together. After much consternation, Kelly overlooked the fact that he was the typical tall, dark, and handsome type. She knew he wasn't pursuing her for money, since her job as corporate pilot provided her only income and her small Cessna was her only asset other than her mother's Nordic stature and coloring. So when he proposed, she accepted. Both career-oriented, they agreed to set the date after Uncle Dan's retirement when Ken became Custom Aero's president, which was supposed to happen at the end of the month.

"Cessna seven-niner-zero, how ya doin'!"

Kelly grinned and took up the mike in her hand. "I just can't sneak up on you guys, can I?" She had forgotten she had turned on her transponder, a device which automatically let the tower know her identification and location. "Cessna seven-niner-zero responding. Are the friendly skies crowded today?"

"We got Citation one-zero-six in the air, but you got plenty of clearance, sweetheart. It's a pluperfect day. Come in any way your little heart desires."

"They're finished, are they?" Kelly shot back,

referring to Ken's latest accomplishment: a modification of a Citation twin turbojet such as the corporation used, which needed a loading bay for light equipment transport.

"Testing her out. You're all clear."

"Keep me that way, fellas, I got something to show ya!" Kelly laughed, her melodic voice reduced to monitone static over the airwaves.

She pulled on her safety helmet and fastened the chin strap before flying by the tower and climbing. The special Lycoming engine seemed to growl as Kelly performed an outside loop to perfection and leveled off to fly over again.

"Cessna seven-niner-zero, have you gone bonkers?"

"Am I still clear?" Kelly asked, gaining altitude for a hammerhead stall.

"No, you're nuts!"

She laughed to herself. She knew it was showing off, but she couldn't help it. Besides, Pete Snyder was always so blasé and monotone. There was nothing any of the pilots loved any more than to get him flustered. So intent was her concentration as she put the plane through the paces for a spine-chilling hammerhead stall, she did not pay attention to the Citation requesting clearance for a northwest approach. With the cool demeanor that she was known for, she visually took its position into consideration. In a clipped voice, she picked up the mike.

"Tell lover boy to hold on, Tower."

The thought that Ken would be livid brought a mischievous twinkle to Kelly's eyes. Her pulse raced in excitement at the silence of the powerful engine and the reeling pitch of the descent. To an untrained eye, the fall looked fatal. Then, at the precise moment, Kelly pulled out of it, the Lycoming roaring to life on cue.

"What the . . . !" a static voice thundered over the radio. The other expletives were not fit for the ears of a lady, but having flown over fifteen hundred hours, she had heard all at one time or another.

"Cessna seven-niner-zero coming in Tower. I passed my aerobatics course!" she added in delight.

The clearance was terse. For a moment Kelly frowned. Pete was always a good sport. It struck her odd that he didn't fall in with congratulations when she told him what she had done. The landing was smooth. As she taxied over to the hangar, where she was allowed to keep her private plane, the Citation was making its descent. She left the helmet on, which boasted the graduation from the flight school on the emblazoned decal across the front, and climbed out of her plane.

"You're in for it!" Mickey, one of the hangar mechanics, called out as she waved at him and started jogging off in the direction of the hangar where the Citation was taxiing.

Her khaki jumpsuit moved with each long and graceful step she took, inviting looks of admiration from the mechanics watching her. By the time she crossed the distance, Ken and Doug Stevens, the head mechanic at Custom Aero, were emerging from the plane. At the sight of her, Ken strode angrily ahead of Doug, his fists clenched on either side of his navy blue flightsuit. Just as he reached her, Kelly yanked off her helmet and ran her finger across the label for him to read. He stopped short, unable to check the curse that was already on its way out.

"Oh, stop being such a spoil sport and kiss me," she teased, throwing her arms about his neck and gazing up at his mirrored sunglasses before adding huskily, "I promise I'll make up for scaring you later."

The disgruntled man grabbed her with a little more force than she expected and covered her mouth with his. As Kelly gasped at the intensity of his kiss—she had only meant a buss on the cheek and was not one to openly display this sort of ardent affection in public—he deepened it, invading her mouth with a bold exploration that he had never tried before. From the sudden heated rush that swept through her, it was just as well he hadn't, she thought wildly. It was Doug's laughter that brought her out of her shock enough to push away from her fiance, a crimson flush of indignation coloring her cheeks.

"Ken!" she admonished, flashing a cutting look at Doug that did not alter his amusement.

"Mac, actually, but why bother with small

details at this point?'' The man who was not her fiancé, she realized to her mortification, pulled off his sunglasses to reveal hazy grey eyes that leisurely assessed her five-foot-ten figure in such a way that her whole face soon matched her cheeks.

Kelly was speechless. He was about Ken's height, perhaps a bit taller, and had the same black hair. She should have missed Ken's mustache, she reprimanded herself furiously. But he did have Ken's name tag on. She wished the earth would open up and swallow her. The man surely thought she was an idiot, a brazen one at that.

''Ace, you left yourself wide open for that,'' Doug snickered, barely getting his amusement at her folly under control. ''A lot has happened since you left two weeks ago. This is James Mackenzie, affectionately known to those close enough to kiss him as Mac.''

Kelly swallowed hard and extended her hand. ''I am terribly sorry. I thought you were my fiance . . .''

''My pleasure, Miss . . .''

Kelly took off her glasses and smiled, the last thing she really felt like doing. ''Benson, Mister Mackenzie. Kelly Benson. Is this your aircraft?''

She would try to carry on as if they had met conventionally, yet the shock of their encounter still left her legs weak. This man was dangerous—warning signals flashed in red alert—and experienced with women from the way he had kissed her. Even now, she felt naked under the cool assessment of those grey eyes.

"I'm acting president of Custom Aero until the elections next week, Miss Benson. At which time the Board of Directors election will officially choose me."

Kelly blanched at the news. "What? Where's Ken?" she asked Doug, turning away from James Mackenzie.

"In St. Louis on business," Doug answered, sobering completely. "Like I said, a lot has happened since you left us two weeks ago. Dan had another attack and sent his letter of resignation from the hospital."

"He's alright now?" Kelly asked, forgetting business.

She loved Dan Mooney like an uncle, although there was no blood relationship between them. He had been a pillar of strength for her, even though he did not do any more to support Marta Benson than purchase her stock when she needed to liquidate. Kelly never did understand the cool distance between her mother and Uncle Dan, but had accepted it.

"He's home now . . . still a bit weak," Doug informed her.

With a grim face, Kelly tucked her helmet under her arm. "I think I'll run over and see him." As she started to turn, a hand gripped her arm, restraining her.

"Now, hold on a minute, young lady. I want

to get this little matter of your circus act resolved. What right do you have coming in here, flying like a maniac in a private airport?''

''She's one of the corporate pilots, Mac,'' Doug cut in, sucking in his cheek to stifle his smile at the brief flash of astonishment on his new boss's face.

Kelly had seen it before. Being a female in a basically male profession had had its pitfalls. Chauvinism ran rampant in the hangars and on the airfields, although most of it was good-natured. The fact that she was a willowy blonde with model-like features had not helped her, but her easygoing manner and skill usually overcame it in time.

Instead of the usual biting remark, Mac Mackenzie laughed and it was not one that made Kelly feel at ease. Whatever his private joke was, he was not about to share it. Maintaining his smile, a white, even one against a sun-bronzed face that drew her attention to how attractive his mouth was, he spoke.

''In that case, see me in my office in one hour.''

Kelly would have objected, reminded him that she was not to go back to work officially until the following day, but she had managed to stir up enough trouble as it was. Instead, she shook his hand firmly again.

''Until then, sir,'' she responded in a professional tone, fighting the urge to salute. A picture of his reaction if she did crossed her mind and her lips turned up in amusement as she turned to face Doug. "I owe you one," she threatened, condemning him for permitting her to make a fool of herself.

As she walked away, she was aware that James Mackenzie's eyes were still on her. She was accustomed to men looking at her. Her height alone drew attention. Yet she rarely paid it any heed. Men were men. They had eyes and they stared, but it didn't usually go any further than that. She had a certain aloofness that warned them off. She was not stuck up, by any means. She was always a friendly clown around her comrades of the airways, but she possessed a certain demeanor that was no-nonsense when it came to a typical come-on.

At least she had, she thought miserably, until she invited a perfect stranger to kiss her and promised to make up for startling him later—her boss, no less. My God, what if he was going to fire her! Kelly groaned inwardly as she picked up her suitcase at the hangar entrance where Mickey had left it for her and walked over to the Tower locker room.

As she entered the door, instead of bearing left, which would have taken her to the men's dressing area, she turned right. It was a small room with a couple of metal lockers, a wooden bench, and a tiled shower stall that had been partitioned off from the men's side when she had come aboard as the first female pilot to work for Custom Aero.

She slipped out of her clothing and shoved them into a laundry bag on top of her overstuffed suitcase. Not bothering with a robe, since she was the only one who used the room, she grabbed a towel from the canvas cart near the door, and stepped into the shower. Afterwards, she felt refreshed and as ready to face her new employer as she would ever be. Surely, he would see that she had been qualified to pull those stunts and understand how she had thought him to be Ken.

Ken. The thought of her fiance brought a frown to her face. What on earth must he be feeling now? The position he had been slaving so hard for, putting in late hours when everyone else had gone home, was suddenly usurped by this Mac Mackenzie. He must be desolate. She would need to assure him that as far as she was concerned, the fact that he was still chief engineer made no difference to her. Holding off the wedding had been more his idea than hers anyway. She had gone along with it because it postponed something that, deep down, she still felt uncomfortable with.

Kelly frowned as she buttoned her silk blouse and tucked it in the jeans that had shrunk to skin tightness in the dryer. Mackenzie . . . James Mackenzie. Where had she heard that name, she puzzled, stepping into high-heeled western boots and dismissing her troubled thoughts about marriage as she always did when they began to monopolize her thinking. After all, she was twenty-four, almost twenty-five. In spite of the glamour and thrill of her job, she did want to settle down and have children.

Of course! James "Mac" Mackenzie! Kelly rolled her eyes heavenward and sat down. She had read articles he had authored in flying publications. His wife's firm had been instrumental in developing classified fighting planes for the government. A one-time mercenary fighter pilot, he had flown with Israel's best in the Seven Day War. What would an aeronautical whiz like James Mackenzie be doing at Custom Aero?

It really didn't matter. The facts were he was here, he was her boss, and she was in trouble. Hoping he had a sense of humor, Kelly left her things in her locker and, after a quick comb of her thick, ash blonde hair, pasted a smile on her face to meet her fate.

As she walked through the cafeteria on the first floor of the office complex, Kelly realized that her predicament was not a well-kept secret. Making a mental note to see Doug Stevens suffer, she made a face at the knowing grins that greeted her. She would determine just how funny her situation was after the meeting. Her hair bounced with her walk as she approached the reception desk to find out which office James Mackenzie had taken.

Since it was after four-thirty, Midge, Uncle Dan's secretary, had left for the day, but Kelly followed the sound of someone speaking in a familiar, rich tone that had embedded itself in her memory after only one meeting. Feeling like a

Christian about to enter the lion's den, Kelly took a deep breath and knocked on the door that had been left ajar. Mackenzie's voice halted in midsentence and then raised to beckon her. She saw that he had been talking into a tape recorder when she took the seat he indicated across the cherry desk and she grinned.

"I thought I was interrupting a meeting."

"Just catching up," he explained, his grey eyes flickering over her in approval. Suddenly, they became impersonal and he leaned forward on folded arms. "Miss Benson, that was one of the most ridiculous stunts I have ever had the misfortune to see outside of a circus. There will be no more of that in the future, is that understood?"

Kelly met his gaze equally, refusing to be intimidated. "I knew what I was doing, sir, but as you will," she condescended, her blue eyes becoming hard. She had been over-enthusiastic, she knew, but she didn't like the way he lorded his position over her.

Even with his executive jacket tossed carelessly across the arm of his leather chair and his tailored white shirt pulled open at the collar with his tie knotted halfway down to his trim waist, he was a commanding personality. His black hair was ruffled, apparently from running frustrated fingers through it, yet his stone-chiseled features demanded respect.

"I understand that you keep your private plane here on corporate property," he went on, ignoring her stab at defiance. "You seem to share a special privilege. Why is that?"

"I'm just likable, I guess."

Kelly could have bitten her tongue off. The quip had slipped out before she realized what it was she had said. She needed this job. Equal opportunity or no, it was hard to come by good paying jobs like this if one was a female. She felt like a child as the grey eyes properly reproached her.

"Are you always this glib?"

She held up her hands in surrender. "Wait, please. Just for a moment, put yourself in my position. Your new employer, whom you didn't even know existed, catches you practicing aerobatics on his airfield, even though you took all the required precautions," she put in in her defense, "and when he approaches you, you invite him to kiss you, thinking that he is your fiance, because you did have on Ken's flightsuit . . ."

"I borrowed it to try out the Citation," he injected for the record.

Kelly's face contorted in frustration. "Well, wouldn't you be the least little bit nervous?"

His laugh made her release her breath in relief. "You're as daring on the ground as you are up there, you know that, Kelly Benson?" There was a distinct change in his eyes as the gaze intensified, bringing an irritating color to her cheeks that she did not understand. "And, if you weren't so damned cute about it, you probably wouldn't have a job right now."

He got up and walked around the desk, indicating the interview was over. Kelly hadn't realized how broad his shoulders were. Jumpsuits had a way of exaggerating one's build, but this tapered shirt left no detail to the imagination. She could even see the imprint of the crisp dark hair under the fine weave of the expensive material. Her inadvertent study became another source of embarrassment as she saw in his wryly amused face that it had been noticed.

She knew he was going to try to kiss her. It was instinctive. It was not, however, that knowledge that made her react, but the fact that her pulses were beginning to leap and race through her veins as though she were still in that hammerhead stall. Her hands reached out to rest lightly against his chest and then withdrew as if the warmth of his body had burned them.

"You needn't bother to kiss me to earn my forgiveness for your bullish demands," she blurted out, scoring a victory at the brief registry of surprise in his eyes.

The victory was short-lived. Kelly braced for the offensive as his arms encircled her, pulling her against his hard chest. She closed her eyes and schooled her features to appear cool and composed as his head lowered over hers. Nothing happened. When she could stand it no longer, she opened her eyes ever so slightly, peeking through the slits of her dark-lashed lids. They widened even more as they meet a pair of laughing grey eyes, dancing above her startled face.

Then the laughter was gone and just as quickly, his lips claimed hers in a sensuous assault that nearly brought her strong defenses crashing down. Where she found the strength to impose indifference on her expression and force a cool note to her voice, she did not know. Survival instinct perhaps, she guessed, as he released her.

"Well, now you have that out of your system, we can begin on a normal employer-employee relationship."

"Are you capable of any kind of normal relationship?" he countered, that lazy smile returning to those sense-searing lips.

"Of course, I am. I will expect you to treat me just like you would if I were one of your regular pilots."

"Good. Then I will meet you at the Hangar for a drink at eight tonight."

"I'm engaged!" Kelly protested incredulously.

"You said treat you as if you were one of my pilots. Sometimes we go out and have a drink . . . talk flying. That's exactly what I had in mind since we have the kissing out of our system, as you put it. On my honor!" he swore, holding up his hand as if taking an oath.

Kelly narrowed her eyes warily. "Have you any honor?"

"None. I am totally unscrupulous."

Again, her eyes widened and she began to wonder who was shocking whom. It was a challenge. She could all but see gauntlets in each of his eyes.

Slowly, the corner of her mouth turned up and her lashes dipped in an unintentionally provocative answer as her lips voiced it. "Alright, Mac. Just a couple of guys having a drink."

"Good show," Mac grinned, giving her a hearty slap on her back that Kelly was certain had left a red handprint.

This was going too far, she thought heatedly, yet she kept her silence. She was as adept at out-maneuvering maneuvers as he apparently was at engineering them. She could prove her ability as a pilot and win his respect. As for the sexual over-tones, she hadn't earned the nickname the boys had dubbed her with behind her back for nothing. The Valkyrie, the cold Viking warrior maid, had just begun to do battle.

TWO

A short, stout lady with graying hair shuffled across the sidewalk outside Kelly's apartment as the girl was about to put the key in the lock to enter. Kelly recognized the landlady of the beachside apartment house and waved.

"Hello, Mrs. Brooks. How are you today?"

"I'm terrific, I'm a grandmother six times as of this afternoon!" the lady announced proudly.

"Lisa had her baby!" Kelly knew Mrs. Brooks's youngest daughter had been due with her third child any day.

"A girl!" the grandmother informed her, catching her breath as she climbed up on the redwood decking that was shared by the vacant apartment next to Kelly's.

The apartment building was located across a dual-laned highway from the white sands that led to the warm Gulf waters. A series of concrete walks led from the decks of every two first-floor units to a pool area surrounded on three sides by a parking lot. The pool was fenced-in naturally by a neatly trimmed evergreen hedge bordered by a colorful flower bed Mrs. Brooks took great pride in.

Kelly sat on the edge of her suitcase, since the woman had taken a seat on one of her lawn chairs. "Well, congratulations! Please tell her I'm thrilled for her."

Mrs. Brooks shook her head. "It just don't seem possible. Six grand-younguns! I guess one of these days you an' that boyfriend of yours'll be married and havin' kids. You ought to, you know, good as you are with them."

Kelly had babysat for Lisa's two older children on occasion and thoroughly enjoyed it. Of course, the boy, a chauvinist in the making, at first refused to believe she made a living as an airplane pilot. It wasn't until she produced pictures and diplomas that he accepted the fact with a degree of disgruntled amazement, that was quickly remedied by permitting him to wear a flight helmet and pretending to be his copilot in a fighter plane—actually two kitchen chairs squeezed between the table and wall. His younger sister insisted on being a stewardess, in spite of her brother's objection that fighter planes did not have them.

"Maybe someday. Did you need something?" Kelly asked at last, knowing it was not like the landlady to sit and chat idly. She only carried on conversations over the roar of a vacuum cleaner or while she was weeding flower beds, and her hands were always busy.

Mrs. Brooks's face took on a worried expression. "Kelly, I hate to ask you, but Lisa was such a big help with the cleaning and she needs a week or so off now that she's had the baby."

"I'll be glad to help," Kelly offered, seeing the woman's predicament.

In addition to renting the apartments, as an extra source of income, Mrs. Brooks and her daughter contracted to clean some of them. Kelly's was among them, since her flight scheduling was not always regular and the last thing she felt like coming home to was an untidy apartment in need of cleaning. Domestic chores were not among her favorite pastimes.

"All I need is some help in this building. If you could do your unit and the adjoining one, it would be a big help. Mary Cannon is going to take the other two."

"You know I will. I'm glad I can help out," Kelly assured her upon seeing the dismay on the woman's face. "Do you have this one rented?" she asked. It had been vacant when she left for her vacation.

Mrs. Brooks laughed and winked wickedly. "A real looker!"

"Why you devil! Here you are a grandmother and lining yourself up, are you?" Kelly teased.

"Just because I'm fifty-three don't mean I can't appreciate a handsome man when I see one!" Mrs.

Brooks snapped with mock indignation. "His name is Mackenzie."

Kelly gasped. "James Mackenzie?"

Mrs. Brooks' eyes narrowed thoughtfully. "Maybe . . . I coulda swore he said to call him Mac." She looked at Kelly. "You know him?"

Kelly nodded in resignation. "He's my boss."

"Lucky you!"

"Strictly my boss, Mrs. Brooks. You know I'm engaged," Kelly reminded her gently. "I'm supposed to meet him tonight at the Hangar . . . for business!" she added, seeing Mrs. Brooks' eyebrows raise.

"I bet that fiance of yours'll just love that," the woman observed. Mrs. Brooks put her hands on the chair arms and shoved herself upright. "Course, if I was as young and pretty as you are, I'd keep both of 'em on a string!"

"You are wicked!" Kelly snickered, getting up and sliding the patio door open to enter.

"I don't have enough energy to be wicked anymore, dear. I just think about it!" the lady retorted, eyes crinkling at the corners. "I really appreciate your help . . . you say you're going to see him tonight?"

Kelly nodded curiously.

"How about givin' him this spare key. He asked me to make it and I hate just leavin' it in the mailbox or goin' in his apartment when he ain't there."

"Sure." Kelly took the key and dropped it into

the change section of her wallet. "Now, you give Lisa my love . . . and the kids, too, if you see them."

"I'll do it, sweetie." The landlady was already making her way down the sidewalk. "You have a good time and remember what I said!"

"I will!" Kelly laughed.

It seemed she was destined to see more of Mac Mackenzie than she had anticipated, she thought as she tossed her purse on the table that separated her kitchenette from the living area. A glance at her watch told her she had an hour before her appointment—it was not social—with her new employer. Her visit with Uncle Dan had lasted longer than she had thought it would.

Kelly had gone straight from her encounter with Mac Mackenzie to the swanky subdivision where Dan Mooney lived. She found him sitting in his living room, television on, feet propped up on an ottoman, with his eyelids closed. In spite of the fact that he had been snoring when she entered the room, he swore that she had not interrupted his nap. Uncle Dan, as Kelly had called him ever since she could remember, had been delighted to see her. When she broke the news to him about finishing aerobatics training, he had shaken his head in consternation.

"Sweetheart, you just put one more block between you and that fiance of yours."

"I don't understand," Kelly answered, a frown

furrowing her smooth brow, ash blonde bangs almost covering it.

"I want to see you happy, Kelly. Ken is a good man, but . . . do you want the truth?" Uncle Dan's eyes searched her face for her answer that came as a nod. "You're too good for him."

"Uncle Dan!"

"No, not socially," Dan Mooney spoke up quickly. "You're too good a pilot. Ken's got a lot of pride. He thinks you are going to don a gingham apron and have a dozen children while he works and brings in the bacon. That's what men like Ken Hudson expect."

"But he knows I'm a pilot and someday I will want kids!" Kelly protested. "And he is so considerate and thoughtful . . ."

"And boring . . . at least for a girl like you."

Kelly frowned. "What's that supposed to mean?"

"Sweetheart, you would eventually become disillusioned with him. You need a man who can best you . . . one you can look up to."

"You know," Kelly grinned, climbing to her feet and crossing to hug the man who had been like a father to her. "You may be a genius on finance, but your expertise where women are concerned leaves much to be desired." She bussed his pale cheek. "I love you, anyway. As a matter of fact, if I were older, I wouldn't look at any other man except you."

Her placating words brought Uncle Dan as

much of a belly laugh as her rendition of her first meeting with Mac Mackenzie did. Instead of being indignant that his successor had nearly barred her from the airfield, he seemed pleased. The fact that he was also her neighbor seemed a hilarious twist of fate to him. When he had finally sobered, he revealed the reason Mac Mackenzie was now president of the corporation—he had bought fifty-one percent of the stock. A buyout was something Ken had never considered.

At least that was one mystery solved, Kelly mused, staring at the clothing hanging in her closet. She picked out a knit jumpsuit and started to toss it on the bed when she reminded herself that this was not a date. If she dressed too provocatively, it would appear as though she was trying to impress him. Certainly she was not, she decided, putting the garment back. Mac Mackenzie was her boss—no more, no less. She would wear the jeans and blouse she had on.

The Hangar was a giant warehouse turned nightclub near the airfield. It was frequented by members of the local flying community, as well as tourists from the beach area. Located on the beach highway, its balcony windows overlooked the shimmering waters beyond luminous white sands. On Friday and Saturday nights, live music was played on an elevated stage in the center of the room, directly under a World War I fighter plane that was suspended from the high ceiling. Flashing lights giving laser effects usually darted around

the room. On the other nights, a jukebox entertained the crowd that gathered to talk and play
billiards or video games at the opposite end of the
building from the bar.

As soon as Kelly's eyes adjusted to the lower
light in the room, they had no trouble picking out
Mac Mackenzie from the others at the bar. Compared to them, he was a good half a head above
the tallest one. He apparently had not bothered to
change in order to impress her either because he
still wore the business suit he had had on earlier,
less the jacket and tie. He leaned on the bar, talking earnestly with a group of young men closer to
Kelly's age, who did not miss her entrance and
whistled for her to join them.

As she approached, she recognized them as reg-
ulars. It was not unusual for her to come by the
Hangar to unwind with her fellow flyers after getting in from a late trip. The subject of flying
always fascinated her, long after her girlfriends
had either found dancing partners or left. She usually left alone, much to many a young male pilot's
disappointment.

"Hey, Ace!" one of the guys spoke up, slapping her on the back as she reached them. "I hear
you're up for a job in a circus. Congratulations!"

Kelly grinned sheepishly, her eyes traveling to
Mac Mackenzie. Ordinarily she would have had a
ready quip, but for some reason her mind was not
working quickly enough.

"Does everyone here know about my little fiasco? I know everyone at the plant does."

"You don't think Dougie boy is going to let you live that down, do you, Ace?" her amused friend remarked, exonerating Mac Mackenzie from her suspicious look.

"And where is Dougie boy?" Kelly asked, glancing about the room. "I have a score to settle with him."

"In a hot game of pool with Keris. Can I get you a drink?"

"I have already spoken for that honor, gentlemen. This is the lady I was waiting for," Mac spoke up, linking his arm in Kelly's to the chagrin and astonishment of the group.

"What'll it be, Kelly?" the bartender asked, curiously eyeing the couple.

"The usual, Jim."

"Make that two!" Mac called out over his shoulder, his hand firmly placed at the small of her back as he guided her to a nearby table.

The air-conditioning was always over-cool in the early hours of the evening and the warmth of his touch seemed intensified. If she had thought about it, she would have brought along a light jacket. A sidelong glance toward the bar confirmed her suspicion that they were being watched, and she was certain Ken would hear about this the minute he touched down on the strip. She sighed. It didn't matter. She had always managed to handle her fiance and he had no reason to be concerned.

"Are you tired?"

Kelly looked up in surprise. "Oh, no!" she smiled, her eyes sparkling in such a way as to deny his question. "I was just thinking that the guys will tell Ken and . . ."

"You're boyfriend is the jealous sort, eh?"

"Not exactly," she replied, wrinkling her small, upturned nose. "He knows my job requires me to be around men."

"Well, if he isn't, he's not normal or he's a fool," Mac remarked wryly, his raking study of her bringing a flush to her cheeks.

"Are you flirting with me?"

"Not at all. I never flirt with my pilots," he evaded suavely, taking the drinks the waitress brought over and placing one in front of Kelly. As he took a sip, he grimaced and shook his head in revulsion. "My God, what is this?"

"Lime and tonic," Kelly laughed, shaking her head so her blonde hair bounced in emphasis of her amusement. "I don't drink . . . at least on work nights," she confessed.

Mac's lips twisted in a grin. "I should have guessed." He caught the waitress before she got away and ordered himself another drink. "Since you're flying me tomorrow, I don't have to worry about a clear head until we get to Dallas."

"Equipment-Aire?" Kelly guessed. Equipment-Aire was a company that sold farms and ranch-oriented aircraft, and one of Custom Aero's better customers.

"That's right. They want a modified cargo plane, lightweight, that is. Bales of hay will be the usual cargo, I imagine."

Kelly smiled mischievously. "You're going to love this account. Monica Peters looks like your type."

Monica Peters was the daughter of the owner and very much involved in the operation. She reminded Kelly of a fashion model because she had never seen the woman with a hair out of place or a wrinkle in her expensive clothing.

"You know Monica Peters, then," Mac answered with a half-smile, inadvertently confirming Kelly's speculation.

"And so, apparently, do you."

Mac's smile widened. He took his second drink from the waitress and gave her a large bill, leaving the change for a handsome tip. Kelly took his lime and tonic for seconds, absently toying with the lime until she became aware of the lazy grey regard of her companion.

"I'm just curious. What exactly is my type?"

"Oh, you know, sophisticated and elegant. They drink champagne, like so . . ." she demonstrated, her pinkie lifted as she tipped the almost empty glass of tonic.

Kelly was taken by surprise as the ice, which had clung to the bottom of the tall, frosted glass, suddenly broke loose and struck her in the nose, some of it escaping from the glass and dropping straight down the front of her blouse. Her face colored as she slapped her hand to her chest, trapping the renegade cube between her breasts and holding it there uncomfortably until it melted.

"I'd never noticed that before." Mac's deep voice was rich with amusement, yet he schooled his features to hide it, pretending he hadn't noticed her predicament.

When Kelly removed her hand, a small dark spot gave evidence that the ice had melted. She glanced down in dismay and then, upon meeting dancing grey eyes, giggled, throwing propriety to the wind, "Oh, well, that's what I get for cutting up."

She wondered what Monica Peters would have done, had the same thing happened to her, and then giggled again. Monica's neckline was usually so low, she could have simply flicked it out. Kelly blushed guiltily and returned her gaze to Mac, aware that he knew she enjoyed a private, and most likely catty, joke. She couldn't help herself. She could not stand Monica Peters. It grated her to be nice when the woman was such a master of sugarcoated insult.

"So, you own fifty-one percent of Custom Aero now," she spoke up, trying to shift the conversation to her companion. "Why didn't you buy up the other forty-nine?"

His initial reaction raised one dark eyebrow. "I tried, but Dan wouldn't sell."

"Dan?" Kelly prompted, thinking it odd that he should be on such a familiar basis with the president of the corporation.

"I've known Dan Mooney for about ten years through the business, I knew your father, too."

It was Kelly's turn to show surprise. "Really?"

"I've got every book he ever wrote on aeronautical engineering. He was a genius."

The genuine praise warmed Kelly because worship could not adequately describe the way she had felt about George Benson. One of the biggest arguments she and Ken had ever had was over his work. Ken had carelessly made the comment that her father was too off-the-wall with his ideas. Kelly rested her hand on his as she met Mac's gaze.

"Did you fly together . . . I mean, how did you know Daddy?"

A flicker of emotion in the grey eyes made her withdraw her hand with an apologetic smile. "Dan and your father were working on a military project and I was the test pilot. A fascinating team, those two. They don't make them like that often."

"Or ever. I think they broke the mold," Kelly confessed, her face darkening briefly. Ken came close, her conscience spoke up in her fiance's defense. At least he wasn't a womanizer.

"Do I detect a daddy's girl or a decided dislike of the opposite sex in general?"

"Not dislike, mistrust is more like it," Kelly

answered wryly. "Particularly of tall, dark, and handsomes."

Mac studied her intently, noticing the dip of her lashes as she concentrated on the skewered lime. "You seem a bit young to be so cynical. I didn't figure you to have that much experience with men."

The lashes flew up curiously. "And you are so experienced you can tell?" The direction of the conversation was not one Kelly liked, mainly because she sensed that this man probably did know a lot about women. It was like having one's soul bared to those haunting grey eyes.

He gave her a careless shrug of indifference. "I've been around. At any rate, it appears one guy must have treated you rather badly."

"Not me . . . my mother," Kelly corrected with a hint of bitterness. "He took advantage of her vulnerability and my father's half of the company."

"And that's why you're so bitter?"

Kelly flushed. "Over his cruel destruction of my mother, not the money!"

"Ah," Mac mused aloud. "So, money doesn't mean anything to you? You are a rare bird, indeed." His grin took the offense out of the remark.

"Well," she grinned back. "I do have to eat. However, I prefer to earn my own keep on my own merit. An inheritance isn't necessary."

"How very idealistic!"

Kelly gave him a playful punch. "Now who's being cynical? Tell me about your wife. I read somewhere that you were married and worked for her father's firm."

She leaned forward on her elbows to listen, pleased at the quick change of topic. It was her turn to be inquisitor. She realized upon seeing a guarded expression cross his face that she had blundered.

"Do I detect a contempt for the blissful institution of marriage or a general dislike of the opposite sex?" she paraphrased, trying to inject some humor into an obviously sore subject.

"Not dislike, mistrust . . . especially the beautiful ones."

Kelly lifted her drink and touched her glass to his. "Touché!"

"And, I am divorced. You must have read an old publication," Mac replied, sipping his drink thoughtfully.

"And you had such a bad experience that you are out to exact revenge on us poor women, using us to amuse yourself without developing strings of attachment," she quipped recklessly.

One corner of his mouth turned up, almost reaching a smile. "Not you, Miss Benson. You're one of the guys."

Good. Now that they had gotten that straight, she might enjoy getting to know Mac Mackenzie as an employer and neighbor.

"Oh, I almost forgot . . ." Kelly broke off as

she searched through her purse for the key. Finding it, she took it out and handed it to him.

"You want a roommate?" he asked in surprise.

"Just a building mate. Mrs. Brooks asked me to give you the extra key you asked for. Your apartment is next to mine," she explained. "And since her daughter just had a baby, I'm helping her out cleaning for at least one week. Would Saturday morning suit you?"

"Will wonders never cease!" He chuckled before answering. "Sure, but just in case I go to the plant early, you better keep the spare key till then," he suggested, pushing it back across the table.

There was a commotion of giggles at the entrance of the club as Kelly returned the key to its place. Upon glancing up, she saw a group of her girlfriends from the volleyball team she subbed for coming in. Thursday night, of course, she reminded herself. They always had a game on Thursday and this was either the victory celebration or the losers' consolation. She waved as they spotted her and started toward the table.

"Kelly, did you pass your course?" one of them asked, rushing up to the table in a stretch terry short-short outfit that accentuated her bounce. Long lashes dropped curiously at the man seated beside Kelly and then back to her expectantly.

"I did. Kaye Phippin, this is Mac Mackenzie, my new employer at Custom Aero."

Kelly went through the introductions and felt an

odd resentment when Mac asked the group to join them. After all, he had said he wanted to talk about flying and that was one thing this crowd knew nothing about.

"Don't you know Kelly and Sue here are off limits, Mr. Mackenzie?" Kaye asked coyly, her brown eyes leisurely taking in the tall frame of the man next to Kelly.

Mac flashed a devastating smile at the girl that made Kelly's toes curl. Boy, what an operator when given the chance, Kelly thought.

"I know that my pilot here is, but don't tell me this lovely creature is, too?" he exclaimed, his eyes traveling to Sue James, Doug Stevens's fiance and Kelly's best friend.

Sue and Doug were to be married the following week and Kelly was going to be the maid of honor. Appropriately enough, Ken was to be Doug's best man. The couple had teased them that they should make it a double wedding, but neither Kelly nor Ken took up the suggestion.

"I'm afraid so, Mr. Macken . . ."

"Mac, please."

"Mac," Sue conceded shyly, her pale green eyes alight at his admiration. "Is Doug here?" she asked Kelly, diverting her attention.

"I hear he's over there at the tables."

"However, you can feel free to ask any of the rest of us out whenever the desire should strike you, Mac," Kaye continued with her usual play. "I, for one, am not shy."

Kelly was not surprised when Kaye pulled out a card with her telephone number and address on it, and presented it to the handsome man next to her. The business cards with her boutique insignia gave all the necessary information to line up a date and also served to let them know she was financially independent and liberated. Equally aggressive on the team, Kaye was a valuable player and, while Kelly did not particularly agree with her solicitation of men, she found the divorcée likable and a lot of fun in a group.

"Down, girl. You'll just have to share him!" another player they had nicknamed Spike, for her obvious prowess at the net, chirped facetiously. Spike was as tall as Kelly, but much thinner with short close-cropped hair and large brown eyes. She always teased Kaye mercilessly over men, yet Kaye was a good sport about it. "Kelly, when are you going to fly us to Acapulco? Would you let her take the corporate plane so we all wouldn't have to fit in that one little seat she has to spare?" Spike said suddenly to Mac, brushing short brown bangs out of her eyes.

"Maybe if we take him with us," Kaye suggested, working an arm through Mac's.

"It's a thought," he grinned, glancing mischievously at Kelly. "You know, hanging out with you could prove to be a real plus. It's like having a good-looking buddy."

"You don't need someone else to draw women to you, Mac Mackenzie, and you know it," Kaye injected. "We all have a good time when we go out. I think you'd like a Mexican holiday with us."

"I'll bet you do," Mac observed. "I'm not sure I could keep up with you."

"What about it, Kelly?"

Kelly shook her head. "Maybe next year. I just took my vacation and, girls, my vacation fund is kaput."

"You spent it all on those flying lessons?" Kaye exclaimed in horror.

"And fuel, Kaye," Kelly reminded her practically.

"Hey, don't forget practice Saturday," Spike reminded Kelly.

Every Saturday, as many of the team as possible gathered at the beach across from the apartment for sun and volleyball. Kelly's abode nearby served as an excellent place to shower and change.

"And girls'-night-out next Friday after the rehearsal!" Kaye added. "I'm taking care of the entertainment just for you, Susie!"

A general groan of mock dismay ran through the group. Early that Friday evening was the wedding rehearsal and dinner for Susie and Doug. Afterward, the guys were taking Doug out and the gals were taking Susie out.

"Just remember, Kaye, I'm getting married the next day and would like to be able to stand up in front of the minister," Susie chided gently.

Kelly snickered, knowing the surprise Kaye had

cooked up for Susie. The shy girl would be shocked, to say the least, when they went out to dinner and a show and the male dancers began to take off their clothes. She had been against it at first, but the thought of Susie's reaction was enough to make her go along with it. She hadn't admitted to the others that she herself had never seen such a show.

Although she hated to leave just when the girls were getting wound up, Kelly was beginning to feel the strain of the long day and wanted to be fresh for the trip tomorrow. She placed her hand on Mac's arm to draw his attention from one of the stories Spike was telling about the night's game as she rose from the table. His other arm went around her shoulder, pulling her closer so he could hear her above the laughter of her friends and the jukebox that had been fired up at the bar. The distinct scent of his aftershave assaulted her nostrils, inviting a stroke of the clean, angular jawline. With a mental shake, Kelly cleared her voice and spoke.

"I'm going to leave you in good company and call it a night. Should I show up with aspirin and a Bloody Mary at the plane tomorrow?" she teased.

"How about if I follow you home . . . since we're almost living together," he added lowly.

"Not necessary. If I come here alone, I usually leave that way," Kelly came back familiarly, disturbed by the way their sudden closeness made her blood warm and cheeks color. "Thank you for the drinks."

As she walked away, she heard Kaye's silky voice. "That's why I get all the guys. Kelly warms them up and I take them home."

Kelly's face was crimson as she waved absently to some fellow pilots at the bar and exited, her purse slung over her shoulder. Perhaps she should have stayed. It was hard to imagine what that crazy bunch would tell him. Not that it mattered, she reasoned. Their relationship was one of business. As she climbed into her 1957 Thunderbird, a relic that she was restoring a little at a time as cash would allow, that fact bothered her more than she cared to admit. With a troubled expression, she buckled her seatbelt for the ride home.

THREE

Mac was already at the airfield by the time Kelly arrived for work. Dressed in a crisp light-blue business suit, he was extremely attractive. The pastel color accentuated his rugged tan and dark features. Alert grey eyes, which quickly assessed her as she sauntered over in her khaki jumpsuit with the Custom Aero insignia to where he and Doug were going over some blueprints, suggested he had not stayed out much longer than she had, although she did not hear him come in. Somehow, that thought pleased her.

"Good morning, Kelly."

"Morning! Are you about ready?"

"In a few minutes." Mac glanced at his watch and smiled as if impressed that she had been punctual.

"I'll check things out and go on aboard, then," she offered in a professional tone.

"Hold up. Take these cases of prints with you.

I'll be working on these," Mac said, indicating the plans in his hands, "but you can carry on the others."

Kelly stopped and stared at the large print cases blankly. It wasn't until she saw a certain twinkle in Mac's eye that she realized she was being tested. Neither Uncle Dan, nor any of the engineers she shuttled, ever expected her to carry their cases. Although if she were a male, more than likely it would have been expected.

"You did ask for no special privileges."

"Ken coming in tonight?" Doug cut in, saving her the exercise of making a witty retort which she somehow could not find.

Instead, she gave a smile that would melt sugar. "Yes. We're going to dinner later. Oh, and don't tell him about my passing aerobatics. I'd like to surprise him. Where do you want these, sir?" Kelly asked Mac, hauling up a case in each hand.

"Anywhere. Just so you can get to them easily when you have to unload them in Dallas."

"You're not planning anything like you did the first time you took Ken up, I hope," Doug snickered, carrying on their conversation.

Kelly's eyes never left the challenging grey ones, in spite of Doug's reference to the first time she met Ken. He insisted on sitting up in the cockpit with her and became a little more frisky than she cared for. When he suggested she become a member of the Mile High Club, if she was not already, Kelly had given him a flight he would not soon forget. He was almost white when she put down on the airfield.

"No, not unless he misbehaves!" she added mischievously, turning to carry the cases to the twin turbojet waiting on the field.

She went through her pre-flight check after stowing the cases, which had been more bulky than heavy, and by the time she was in her shoulder harness and seatbelt, Mac joined her. To her chagrin, he chose to sit in the copilot's seat instead of in the passenger area.

"I promise to behave myself," he grinned as he fastened up for the takeoff. "While there may be nothing more esoteric than intimacy at five-thousand two-hundred-eighty feet, I prefer my pilot's attention focused on his or her flying."

Kelly's cheeks were a becoming shade of pink as she received clearance from the tower and made a smooth takeoff. That was two she owed Doug Stevens, she vowed silently at his having told Mac about her first flight with Ken. Her outer appearance was one of cool professionalism, but clammy palms, which she kept drying on her pant legs, betrayed her inner discomfort at having Mac MacKenzie in the cockpit with her. It was worse than having her flight instructor. Although she was an excellent pilot, Mac was renowned for his ability in almost any type of aircraft and it was intimidating.

They were ordered to a holding pattern over Dallas for twenty minutes before she finally got clearance from the controller to come in. As she taxied past the commercial planes, she felt as if she were in a toy compared to their size and power. She kept her eyes and ears open, appreciating Mac's help in all the congestion. Even though the controllers were alert and did an excellent job, there was always the chance that someone would not listen to their instructions, which meant the other planes had to be alert for those in too much of a hurry to wait for the controller's go-ahead.

The flight had not been nearly as bad as Kelly had first thought. Like the night before, Mac had a way of getting her to talk. When she wasn't telling him about her flight instruction, he entertained her with some stories of his own experiences. He was one of the most fascinating people she had ever met and when they reached their destination, Kelly was almost disappointed.

As Mac promised, she had to carry the cases across the airfield to the terminal building where she handed them over to a taxi driver whom Mac had engaged to take him to the Equipment-Aire complex. He left Kelly with instructions to meet him back at the plane at five.

She didn't show her dismay until the cab pulled away with him and then made a juvenile face at the direction he took. Ken was due back at Custom Aero this afternoon and their dinner date was for six. With a resigned sigh, she found a pay phone and left a message with Ken's secretary that it would be eight at the earliest before she could make it.

The day passed quickly. Kelly was never bored in the skyscrapered city. Old City Park was one of her favorite places to spend time. Pioneer buildings of the past, preserved by those who treasured it and took pride in it, provided hours of sightseeing that she never tired of. From there, she sought out the log cabin where Neely Bryan, founder of Dallas, had lived in on Elm Street. The rustic one-room log building was an oddity against the background of modern ones.

A late lunch at the European Crossroads Cafe near the artists' market of the Olla Podrida completed her step into the past. The old world atmosphere made her expect to see a mustached Sam Houston step into the vined courtyard where she enjoyed a shrimp salad with the house dressing. She stared dreamily at the balcony with descending steps to the tiled floor below where wrought iron furniture and red-checkered tablecloths gave it a romantic air. Broad-leafed trees growing up through the center provided ample shade from the hot Texas sun beating down on the city.

Kelly closed her eyes and pictured her imaginery companion across from her and was startled when Mac Mackenzie's face appeared instead of her fiance's. Shaking herself mentally, she opened her eyes. A soft laugh emerged from her throat when she saw that she did indeed have a luncheon companion. A small bird had perched warily at the opposite end of her table. Carefully, so as not to spook it, Kelly tossed it a bread cube and smiled as it greedily took its expected treat and flew away.

The rest of the afternoon was occupied by idly milling through the artists' market. Ingenious creations fascinated her and she felt an occasional twinge of envy at the vast display of talent there. There were two levels decorated with brightly-colored canopies and multi-leveled balconies, constructed in warm wood, not the usual metal and chrome decor of most malls. All were hung, almost to the point of litter, with baskets, hammocks, and other handmade crafts. She left with a few hand-dipped candles and a bouquet of fresh flowers wrapped for travel in a bag that would seal moisture around the stems until she could put them in water at home.

She was back at the airport by four-thirty. After making sure the plane was refueled and ready for takeoff, she returned to the air-conditioned terminal to wait for Mac.

Five o'clock came and went, as did six. At seven, she attempted to call Custom Aero to see if Ken might still be there, but the night watchman told her everyone had gone for the weekend. Ken's answering machine was on at his place, so she could only guess that he might have gone to her apartment. But there was no answer there, either. Reluctantly reconciled to the idea that she could not reach him, she checked at the informa-

tion desk for messages and then she walked back
to her seat to wait for her employer, her ire fueling
with each passing minute.

It was eight o'clock when she caught sight of
his commanding figure among a rush of people
making their way toward the gate of the flight just
announced over the speaker. A smile, white
against his tanned face, made him particularly
attractive, but did nothing to dent the irritation
Kelly felt. If he had been tied up on business, the
least he could have done was leave a message at
the information desk at five when she was sure to
be at the airport.

As the departing passengers left him at the busy
gate, Kelly noticed that he was not alone. A petite
brunette in a well-tailored linen suit and a cowl-
necked silk blouse walked beside him. So, that
was who that smile was for, Kelly mused grudgingly. As usual, Monica Peters was striking, drawing more than one glance of admiration as she
glided by gracefully on three-inch designer heels,
her arm linked possessively in Mac's. She stared
up at him in utter fascination with whatever he
was talking about. A single strand of pearls, a
shade lighter than the hot pink of her suit, lay in
the valley of her full bosom covered enticingly by
the clingy drape of silk.

Lips the same shade tightened Monica's smile
as she saw Kelly standing by the door to the steps
leading down to the field where the Citation
waited, ready to go. There was no love lost

between them. It was no secret that Ken had dated Monica for a year before he met Kelly. He had even proposed to her, but he was entirely too serious for a woman like Monica Peters to settle down with. Although the rejection was of her own making, Monica took the news of Kelly's engagement to Ken as a personal affront and had acted with barely suppressed hostility ever since. The frequent patronage of Monica's father's firm with Custom Aero constantly brought her to the plant and it grated Kelly to have to submit passively to her sugarcoated barbs. But, after all, she was the customer.

"Well, well, are you still wooing that drab little engineer, Kelly?"

Ignoring the jibe, Kelly held out her hand. "Hello, Monica. Good to see you again," she said with a forced smile before turning her attention to the man who watched them curiously. "I'm sorry, sir, but I thought you said we were to leave at five o'clock." Although her voice was appropriately respectful, her eyes were hard as they met the grey ones.

"Did we keep you waiting, Kelly?" Monica exclaimed in an unfelt apology. "It's my fault, I'm afraid. Mac and I haven't seen each other in such a long time and I was absolutely famished after that long meeting, so . . ."

"I apologize, Kelly," Mac cut in. "I did leave a message at the information desk, but the lady who took it could barely speak English. I was afraid you hadn't gotten it when you didn't show up.''

"But she would have felt like a third wheel anyway, darling."

"No problem, sir. I'll take that." Kelly reached for the case Mac carried in his right hand. At least he had only brought back one.

Mac's grip tightened on the handle under her own fingers. "I'll take it. It's the least I can do."

There was an apology in his eyes. They held Kelly's obstinately until hers softened. Monica was a customer, she reasoned in his defense. Perhaps that was all there was to it, although it really didn't make any difference. Kelly shrugged and led the way down the steps to the runway where the turbojet waited to leave. As she took her place in the cockpit, she saw Monica approaching in the reflection of the glass. Kelly glanced over her shoulder in time to see Monica close off the cockpit from the passenger section with a sly wink. On the other hand, they were probably about to renew an old relationship, Kelly surmised. Switching to her professional role, she mentally dismissed the entire subject to contact the controller for clearance to take off.

The flight back was uneventful. Occasionally Kelly heard laughter from the couple in the back. The clink of glass and ice indicated that they were having a private party and she was glad Monica had closed the heavy curtain. Kelly concentrated more heavily on her instruments, keeping an alert eye for any lights that might indicate another air-craft in the skies at her altitude.

When she finally got home after leaving Monica and Mac to decide where to spend the remainder of the evening, Ken was not at the plant, at his apartment, or at her place. She did, however, find a note on her dining room table that told her he had been there and, after a two-hour wait, had given up on her. It was signed simply, "Ken," which also told her that he was not in a good humor.

In frustration, she wadded the note into a ball and hurled it into the trash can. As if it were her fault, she thought heatedly. It wasn't as if she had enjoyed sitting at the airport for three hours while Mac and Monica wined and dined. Men! Some-times she wondered why she even bothered with them.

FOUR

Ken's call woke Kelly early Saturday morning. When she explained what had happened, his irritation shifted to their new employer with such force that Kelly was taken by surprise. From the undercurrents, she realized that Ken had not taken losing his chance for corporate president very well at all. She tried to assuage him as much as possible, drawing possibilities from her sleepy thoughts. Surely Mac would recognize Ken's potential and, since Mackenzie was known to take over companies and reorganize them before moving to greater challenges, perhaps he would leave the position to Ken then.

Her attempt was not successful. She'd hung up after an invitation for a day at the beach with the volleyball gang and a quiet dinner at her apartment later which he accepted readily. He'd not only sounded upset, but very tired as well, and Kelly hoped the lazy day would be the prescription he needed to restore his usually good humor.

She took out a roast beef from the freezer to thaw and donned a pair of worn cutoff jeans and an oversized T-shirt to tackle the cleaning she'd promised to do for Mrs. Brooks. Her own tidy apartment did not take very long, so she started on it, saving Mac's until later to give him time to sleep off his night on the town with Monica. Although she should buzz right in and make ungodly amounts of noise to get even for his lack of consideration last night, even if it did appear to be inadvertent, she thought vindictively.

When her own place was spic and span, she loaded her cleaning supplies in a bucket and dragged the canister vacuum cleaner by its hose across the redwood deck to Mac's apartment. Her knocking produced no answer. The opaque curtain had been drawn, making it almost impossible for her to make out any movement inside, yet the odd shapes she did make out were still. A quick glance around the parking lot did not reveal the Mercedes sports car he drove. So, recalling his saying that he might go in to work on the weekend, she fished the key he insisted she keep out of her pocket and let herself in—cleansers, sweeper, and all.

Unlike her place, his was still in chaos from moving. Boxes, both full and empty, were shoved against the wall, making a path from the door to the kitchen area with a deviation to the bedroom. A tweed sofa of apricot, beige, and blue with matching chairs furnished the living area, arranged in a semicircle around a low, round oak table. A lovely antique, Kelly noticed with admiration. On the opposite wall, a television and stereo component system had been placed on portable oak wall cabinets, but the wires spewing from the various pieces of equipment indicated that all of it had not been hooked up. The easy listening music that played through the large speakers on either side of the display and a lighted dial indicated, however, that at least the radio worked.

Kelly surveyed the mess—in a dilemma as to what to do first. The boxes either needed to be stacked so that she could vacuum, or unpacked. As she walked through the maze, she saw that some of them contained kitchen utensils. A check in the cabinets confirmed her suspicion that they were empty. Deciding that she could unpack them and be rid of them once and for all, she started in on her task.

She filled the bucket with water and detergent to wipe out the cabinets before unpacking the boxes. If he did not like where she put things, he could always rearrange later, but at least he wouldn't have to fall over them. Besides, he was certainly not a cook extraordinaire because the boxes appeared to contain only the barest essentials to provide a filling meal.

A spill in the back of the cabinet under the sink proved to be stubborn. Kelly crawled into the cabinet, avoiding the pipes with her head as she scrubbed vigorously to get up the sticky substance. A sudden darkening of the already dim light inside the enclosure warned her that she was no longer alone. As she wormed her way backward to get out, she heard Mac's amused voice.

"Well, I never expected to find such an interesting spectacle in my kitchen cabinet this morning," he teased, as she sat down in the middle of the floor.

The cool touch of the linoleum on her backside let her know that her shorts had ridden up to reveal more of her than she would have cared to show. Kelly brushed the mop of blonde curls out of her face and grinned sheepishly.

"I think I got more than I bargained for cleaning this place."

"I think I did by renting it."

Kelly looked up, her cheeks coloring at his meaning. "I thought you were gone . . . I mean, I did knock," she stammered, noting that he wore a bathrobe. A dark stubble on his chin indicated he had just gotten up.

A short laugh relaxed his finely-chiseled features. He combed his fingers through unruly black hair with his hand in an attempt to smooth it. "To tell the truth, I had forgotten you were coming over . . . or that it was Saturday."

"Darling, am I to assume we're not alone?" a voice came from the adjoining room.

"You may, Monica." He didn't seem the least

disconcerted that he was caught in rather embarrassing circumstances.

Kelly, however, felt differently. Her eyes widened in mortification. Monica! Ignoring the way Mac studied her, she dropped her eyes and hurriedly gathered her scattered cleaning supplies.

"I . . . I am really sorry!" she apologized, wanting to get out of the apartment before Monica emerged. "I'll . . . I'll come back later. Perhaps tomorrow, since I'll be busy this afternoon." She wasn't going to let Mac Mackenzie's indiscretions with Monica interfere with her date with Ken again. As long as she cleaned, it shouldn't matter when she did it.

"No, no!" Mac protested, holding up his hand to stop her. "It's my fault. We'll go out for breakfast." One corner of his mouth twitched with humor. "I'm not exactly set up to entertain, anyway."

It didn't stop him last night, Kelly thought peevishly. "Fine," she agreed shortly, turning back to her task after pulling the back of her shorts down primly. Perhaps from her position behind the kitchen counter, the other woman would not notice her.

As if reading her thoughts, Mac headed Monica off and proposed they eat out at the small cafe a block away.

"But who's here, darling?" Monica asked curiously. "Besides, as much as I love you in the altogether, you can't go in your bathrobe," she chided with a sultry laugh.

"It's the day for the cleaning lady," he explained, before adding in a reproachful voice, "And I have my swimsuit on under this, wicked lady, so wait until I get my shirt and we'll leave the lady to her work."

Kelly dove under the cabinet as she heard the light approach of Mac's guest. Her face was flushed with an indignation she could not fathom. This had to be the most humiliating circumstance of her lifetime. She scrubbed where the stain had been until she lifted the shelf paper right off the cabinet floor, not relaxing until she heard Monica's retreating footsteps.

"You haven't changed, darling. I should have known better than to expect you to have a dowdy middle-aged housekeeper," she purred cattily. "I can't wait to hear how you pay her."

"And you haven't changed either, Monica," Kelly heard Mac retort caustically. "But, for the record, Kelly and I have a strictly business relationship."

Kelly groaned inwardly as she heard her identity revealed, but the dismay was cut short by Monica's sharp intake of breath. She was almost disappointed that she could not hear her reply, but Mac had closed the door behind them. A hint of a smile played at her mouth as she resumed her task.

She barely had time to shower before Ken arrived. Mac's apartment was now orderly, or at least his kitchen was. She had unpacked everything that had an obvious place, receiving an odd sense of satisfaction from her efforts. In spite of her unconscious reaction to Mac Mackenzie inviting Monica to spend the night with him, Kelly was anxious for him to see how nice his apartment looked now.

It was more than was expected of the job Mrs. Brooks had asked for, she knew, but it had been fun. With each box she unpacked, she felt that she knew a little more about him. Now, all that remained to be unpacked were pictures and the books that would not fit in the wall cabinet. They were neatly stacked in the living room cloak closet where an overcoat and a few jackets hung.

Kelly didn't bother to blow-dry her hair because she was going swimming. It curled in golden ringlets that bounced when she started to answer the knock at the door announcing Ken's arrival. She stopped long enough to give herself a quick examination in the mirror. She hadn't applied any mascara. It would likely run, leaving her with black eyes the moment she dove into water. Yet, the natural dark color of her eyelashes negated the necessity anyway. She only used what little makeup she did for emphasis. Satisfied that she was presentable, she rushed out into the living room to let him in.

"Well, hello!" Ken exclaimed, his brown eyes alight with admiration as they took in her tall, tanned body garbed in a modest turquoise maillot.

The swimsuit was cut high on the legs and to bikini proportion in the back, making her long legs appear even longer. A lettuce-edged ruffle crossed the fitted bodice held up by spaghetti straps that crossed the back.

"Hello yourself, stranger," Kelly greeted him, stepping up on tiptoe to bestow a welcome kiss.

Not to be brushed off with a friendly buss on the lips, Ken pulled her to him, his hands enjoying the soft exposure of bare skin that enticed him to explore every inch propriety would permit. His lips caught hers and covered them in a warm, but restrained manner.

"Did you miss me?" he asked huskily.

"You two should go inside if this is just the warm up!"

Kelly broke away from Ken at the unexpected intrusion to see Monica leading the way up the wide steps of the deck with Mac Mackenzie behind her. Her face burned as she flashed an openly hostile look at Monica before she regained her composure. How dare she after . . . after . . .

"What are you two doing here?" Ken asked in surprise, his arm snaking possessively around Kelly's waist.

"Hello, Kenneth darling." To Kelly's astonishment, Monica walked up to Ken and kissed him on the cheek.

If her actions annoyed Mac, it did not show. Actually, he seemed amused and that further aggravated Kelly. To think that she had done all that extra work for him!

"I'll go get the towels and blanket," Kelly excused herself, moving Ken's hand away from her with a sharp motion, her irritation growing at the way he stared at Monica's skimpy swimsuit, barely concealed by a black net cover-up.

The towels she used for the beach lay on her bed. She snatched them up and shoved them into the straw carrier angrily. Monica was never satisfied with one man. She wanted them all . . . and Ken was simple enough, even after she jilted him, to openly admire her. Couldn't he see that's exactly what she wanted! Kelly's teeth grated as she hooked her hand in the handles of the bag and took it into the living room.

"I didn't know Mac Mackenzie was your new neighbor."

"What difference does it make?" She could not help the sharpness of her tone.

Ken looked at her for a moment before a satisfied smile crossed his face. "Are you jealous because Monica Peters kissed me?"

"Absolutely not! She'd kiss a dog, if it was male."

"Thanks," he replied flatly.

Gradually, the hair on the back of her neck began to lie back down as she realized how foolish she appeared. It wasn't really Ken. It was the fact that Mac Mackenzie seemed to enjoy her predicament and offered no help in holding Monica in check. After all, he had spent the night with her and just bought her breakfast when she turned on the charm for another man, an ex-fiance at that.

"Actually, I'm the one who should worry . . . a lady killer like Mackenzie practically living with my girl." Ken took her in his arms again. "I don't want you cleaning his place again," he whispered, cutting off her astonished intake of breath with his lips. "And I don't really like you flying him around, but thanks to his low-handed tactics, I don't have much choice . . . unless you'd quit."

"I'm not his type . . . and I'm definitely not quitting my job," she purred, brushing the tip of his aquiline nose with own her lips.

She backed away and took up her beach bag from where she had inadvertently dropped it. "And I'll not clean his place again, unless Mrs. Brooks needs me to."

"That woman takes advantage of your good nature."

"Let's go to the beach, shall we? I think we've hit enough bumps for one day," Kelly quipped, hoping to avoid another confrontation.

Ken did not like Mrs. Brooks. There had been several times when he had wanted to go out, but Kelly had committed herself to helping the lady in one way or another—if not cleaning, then occasionally painting or baby-sitting for her grandchildren. But Kelly felt she was more than repaid by Maggie Brooks's thoughtfulness. So many times she'd received casseroles, fresh flowers from the garden, and extras in the cleaning, such as shampooing the furniture, or a load of laundry washed and folded on her bed. The way Kelly saw it, it all evened out.

The breeze was off the water, just enough of one to keep her from basting in her own sweat. After a quick dip in the water, Kelly fell onto a towel to soak in the sun's penetrating rays, leaving Ken to more athletic swimming beyond the waders and children. She closed her eyes, listening to the sounds of the gulls, the gentle lap of the water against the sand, and the frolic of the kids of all ages that gathered there. It always was a soothing combination, enhanced by a local radio station playing from someone's beach blanket.

She must have drifted off to sleep because she awoke with a startled scream when ice was placed against her lower back. A stampede of bare footpads on the sand surrounded her as she scrambled to hold her top modestly to her chest, having nearly lost it when she bolted upright because she had undone the straps to avoid tan marks.

"Watch it, kid. That'll bring more attention than that scream!" Spike teased, backing away as Kelly threw a handful of sand in retaliation.

"Where's lover boy?" Kaye asked, tucking the strap of her high-cut tanksuit back up on her shoulder.

"In the water."

"Come help us set up, Kelly!" another team

member called out, struggling with the poles wrapped up in the regulation-sized net.

They found an area that was not too heavily populated by sunbathers to set up on. In no time at all, the team was batting the ball back and forth with concentrated coordination. Kelly joined in, waving briefly at her fiance who was drying off near the blanket. Ken never objected to the Saturday afternoon ritual. In fact, he seemed to enjoy talking to any boyfriends that might come along and definitely enjoyed the coaching he was called upon to do at times.

The team worked out for one hour seriously before inviting any interested parties to join. Kelly went in for another swim to cool off before rejoining the group. To her surprise, Mac Mackenzie was standing next to Kaye Phippin. A quick search found Monica sipping a wine cooler and watching the play from a beach lounge nearby. She had taken off her cover-up and now lay stretched out in a shimmering bikini of black with golden threads woven in it. Small gold chains held the front to the back at the curve of her hips and the front of the skimpy halter. It showed her shapely body to perfection, as dark and exotic as her shining black hair.

Kelly started to take a place beside Ken when Kaye called out from the other side. "Our side, Ace! We're short one."

With a helpless shrug, Kelly grinned at Ken's grim face and jogged over to the other side. Her position next to Spike made their front line formidable. She and the other girl were quite a bit taller than the other players, notwithstanding the men. With a toss of blonde curls, bleached whiter by the sun, Kelly turned to wait for Mac to serve the ball.

The sun glistened on his tanned chest as he turned sideways and brought his hand up to send the ball smoothly over the net. It dropped neatly to the other side between two girls who were paying more attention to the server than the serve. Kelly clapped her hands in approval as Kaye jumped up to give him a peck on the cheek.

"Just think what you'll get if you win," she said, winking wickedly as he caught the ball.

"Don't fluster the server, Kaye. You'll muddle his concentration," Spike shouted from the front row.

The second serve dropped right where the first did, but this time the girls were on their toes. A set up and a hit sent the ball to Kelly who set the ball up for Spike. True to her nickname, the girl sent the ball spiking the ground on the other side of the net. Kelly jumped up and down enthusiastically and patted Spike on the back. Ken returned the third serve and after one of Kelly's teammates hit it out-of-bounds, the ball went to his team.

The game ran nip and tuck. Kelly threatened revenge on her fiance when Ken spiked the ball on her, catching her off guard. Kaye kept a close eye on Mac, which delighted Kelly. She could see the sparks flying from the lounging sun queen, whose bottom lip was beginning to protrude in decided petulance. A high serve came across the net in Kelly's direction. Her front man jumped to return it, only to have it shot back. Kelly backed up to set it up.

"Mine!"

She heard Mac's call and tried to halt, but her momentum carried her right into him. He twisted to avoid her and lost his footing as she went down on her back. He came down on top of her in a heap. For a minute, Kelly lay winded by the fall and the weight that kept the air from returning to her lungs. Concerned grey eyes met hers.

"Are you alright?"

His breath was warm against her cheek, but it was the touch of his body, hot and damp, against her own flesh that took her breath away. Mutely, Kelly nodded, unable to tear her gaze away from his.

"This is not a contact sport, guys. Let's go!" Spike reminded them mischievously as she stood over them and held out her hand to Kelly. "Falls are harder on us tall gals, right, Ace?"

"Yes," Kelly laughed nervously as Mac moved quickly to his feet and hooked his arms under hers to help her up. "I . . . I'm sorry. I couldn't stop."

What on earth was wrong with her, she chastised herself as she brushed the sand off her legs briskly. Her hands were almost trembling and her heart was stuck somewhere just above her vocal chords, making intelligent speech hopeless. Guiltily, she glanced at Ken, hoping he had not noticed her discomfiture, but he was glaring at Mac in an openly hostile way leaving little doubt that he thought Mac had planned their collision.

At the end of the game, Ken left to snack on the sandwiches he had brought along. Kelly also excused herself to join him, sensing that another argument would be in the making if she did not follow his lead. He handed her a soda as she dropped down Indian fashion on the towel beside him.

"Hungry?" he asked without much interest.

"Nope, this is all I need right now. I think I'll cool off and then nap a little. If you'll protect me from those ice-bearing pranksters, that is."

"They're not the real threat, but I'll protect you," he promised somberly.

Kelly let the subject drop and handed him back his drink. "I'll be right back."

She jogged out past the shallows where Mac had coaxed Monica in up to her knees. The darkhaired beauty clung to his muscled arm as if in fear of being swept away by the gentle swells that lapped up on the wet sand. If he thought Monica Peters was going to get her hair wet, Mr. Mackenzie had another thought coming, Kelly remarked to herself with a wry grin. She was a sun worshipper, not a beach bather. Her swimsuit was designed for sunning, not swimming. Kelly gave her own damp curls a careless brush with her fingers, dismissing the couple, and diving under.

She swam leisurely back and forth beyond the bathers between the two lifeguard stands she used as markers to gauge her course. Swimming was not only an excellent exercise, but a natural sedative as well. The exertion worked out her muscles and a short rest on the beach permitted the sun to gently massage them into a state of relaxation with its warm rays. She took one last dip and made sure she was free of sand before starting back up to the beach. As she came up, a pair of hands caught her waist, thumbs pressing into the flesh of her back.

"What?"

"It's only me. You were about to swim into me," Mac explained, setting her on her feet, holding her only long enough to see that she had her balance.

Kelly smiled. "I don't open my eyes under water. Sorry!" Monica must have retreated to her chair because Kelly's cursory sweep of the surrounding area did not find her.

"Are you always sorry, Kelly?" Grey eyes narrowed in their study of her.

Puzzled by his comment, she shrugged it off and started to wade away, but his hand restrained her with strong fingers that burned into her arm in spite of their gentle hold. Kelly looked at it before raising her eyes in question.

"Don't you have enough woman trouble already?

Kaye and Monica will be at each other's throats. And frankly, my money's on my teammate," she joked, not really seeing any humor at all to the situation.

"There should be no trouble with you. After all, you're my pilot . . . strictly business," he reminded her, one corner of his mouth lifting cynically.

Kelly's heart stopped for what seemed an eternity as his gaze riveted her to the spot. Surely, he couldn't know how he affected her. He mustn't ever, she thought, at least not until she fully understood it herself. His hand, still on her arm, seemed to burn into her skin, setting it on fire. Her eyes dropped to the crystal droplets of water clinging to the dark curls on his chest and then tore away.

"Yes, sir," she responded with a nervous laugh, lifting her hand in mock salute so that he released his disturbing grasp, but his voice stopped her from moving.

"Look, I apologize if I'm causing any trouble between you and your fiance. I can see he is suspicious over nothing. If there's anything I can do, let me know."

Her heart dropped against her stomach at the impersonality of his statement. Well, whatever it was she was feeling was one-sided and he didn't seem to have any idea, thank goodness. There was an odd mixture of relief and disappointment tearing at her as she nodded in acknowledgment and walked away.

Ken watched her approach, his face revealing his witnessing of her brief encounter with Mac in the water. Kelly forced a smile and sat down beside him.

"Any sodas left?"

"Sure." Ken reached in the cooler and took out a can. "What did he want this time?" he asked as he handed it to her.

"Mac?" She cursed the deepening of her color and hoped the sun she had gotten that afternoon was camouflaging it.

"Who else, sweetheart?"

Kelly took in a deep breath and let it out slowly. "Ken, are we going to spend our whole day arguing over nothing?"

"Let me guess. He apologized for inadvertently coming between you and me, right?"

Kelly's amazed expression betrayed the answer. "How did you know that?"

"Because I am a man and I know those tactics, my sweet little innocent."

Kelly suddenly felt the arm that supported her swept out from under her and found herself on her back with Ken leaning over her. "My drink!" she gasped, looking over her head where the overturned can spilled its contents onto the sand.

"I'll get you another one," he mumbled against her lips, before taking them gently.

"Ken, not here!" she protested, twisting her head to the side.

A wide grin spread on his face. Instead of completing the kiss, he rubbed noses playfully. "You see, sweetheart. I'm a gentleman, in spite of the way I acted when we first met," he added quickly at the rise of her brow. "I'll go along with your pleas to wait, although you make it very difficult for me, you guileless vixen. But if you were in his arms right now, he would take what he wanted."

"A real swine, eh?" Kelly mimicked in a pirate's brogue.

"The pits, me hearty."

A growl that came from neither her mouth nor his made their eyes widen in wonder. Ken laughed and rolled aside, his hand slapping his flat stomach.

"It's me. My stomach rebelled against those soggy sandwiches and starves for that delicious-looking beef that I saw thawing on the counter," he confessed. "Do you think we could cut this short and speed up supper?"

"Sure." Kelly climbed to her feet and brushed the sand off her legs. "I even have some fresh fruit to hold you until it's done. Speaking of upset stomachs," she began mischievously, "I passed my aerobatics training this past week!"

"Why?" The grim question made Kelly regret her words instantly.

She looked around, as if searching for an answer, spotting Mac and Monica watching her from behind dark glasses. She could not see their eyes, but she could feel their curious gaze. Turning to the matter at hand, she shrugged.

"Why not?" she retorted lamely. "It was fun."

"I'm surprised you didn't wait until I was hanging upside down in a loop-to-loop before informing me."

"Oh, Ken," Kelly moaned, leaning over, unaware of the provocative view of her neckline, and taking his face between her hands. "Don't be such a fuddy-duddy! I wouldn't do that to you. At least as long as you act right!" she added impishly, jumping back with a squeal as he grabbed at her.

She snatched up the small cooler and ran out of his reach. "Bring the towels and my bag!" she ordered, her voice rich with amusement. "Beat you to the shower!"

"Go for it, Ken!" Spike shouted from a nearby blanket.

Kelly gasped, dropping the cooler in horror as her hands went to her face. She hadn't meant that. She chanced a look to where Spike grinned delightedly and shook her head in denial. Keep your mouth shut, a voice counseled wisely. The more you say, the worse it will get. Let them have their fun.

"I just can't seem to keep her under control until the wedding," Ken remarked wickedly to the girls on the blanket near the volleyball net. "I'd like to make an honest woman out of her."

"You're horrible!" Kelly accused, beginning to see the humor of her blunder.

"You started it, sweetheart."

As Kelly picked up the cooler, she caught a glimpse of Mac Mackenzie out of the corner of her eye. A straw hat was pulled down over his face where tinted glasses hid his eyes, but the gentle shake of his broad chest betrayed his amusement. With a stiff lift of her chin, she plodded ahead through the sand, her face scarlet. Of all the people, she groaned inwardly. It seemed she was destined to play the fool for that man.

FIVE

The following week passed rather quickly with last minute details for Doug and Susie's wedding being worked in between Kelly's work schedule. She ran several day shuttles to Dallas and Houston, but Mac was only on one of them. Monica must have taken a hotel room for the remainder of her stay in Corpus Christi because Kelly saw no sign of anyone staying with Mac. She'd seen him coming in late, but from the way he was dressed, she knew he had been putting in late hours at the plant. He'd told her he intended to have first-hand knowledge of every project underway and, from the hours he was putting in, she had no doubt that he would.

Kelly found herself admiring Mac's drive. She could see why he was so successful. The general talk in the cafeteria was favorable toward the new boss with the exception of Ken's opinion. Her fiance resented being checked on. Ken took pride in his work and did not like Mac Mackenzie looking over his shoulder. Kelly had pointed out that, since Mac had not made any changes in Ken's prints, he must have been impressed by them and surely that was a compliment. Ken, however, continued to harbor a growing resentment that concerned her.

After a bridal shower on Tuesday night at Kaye's home, Kelly helped Susie put all the gifts away in the apartment she and Doug were going to move into after the wedding. They decorated the private party room of the club on Wednesday and Thursday evening. By Friday, Kelly wasn't sure she could hang in with the girls for the bachelorette party after the wedding rehearsal. Although she'd hated to do it, she asked Mac to make his meeting with his Houston clients as short as possible, so she could get off work no later than five. He had not only done that, but gotten her back an hour early, saying it was the least he could do after holding her up in Dallas the previous week.

Kelly smiled, recalling his thoughtfulness, as she applied a hint of baby-blue eye shadow. Ken was so wrong about the kind of man Mac Mackenzie was. Sometimes her fiance could be stubborn to the point of exasperation. Her nose wrinkled in disgust and then sniffed at the delicious aroma invading her senses. Her stomach growled in response, her luncheon salad at the Houston airport a distant memory. Curious as to where it was coming from, she slipped into a pair of spiked sandals the same color as the backless royal jump-suit she wore. The soft knit clung to her shapely legs as she walked into the living area and peeked outside.

"Well, well! Aren't you something!" Mac observed from his side of the deck where he stood over a smoking gas grill.

Kelly smiled and made a small curtsy. "Why thank you, sir. What are you burning?" She opened the screen and stepped out onto the patio.

"Barbecued shrimp. Sit tight a minute and I'll let you sample one. How about a daiquiri?"

Kelly hesitated a moment and then nodded. "If you have one already made," she stipulated. She had a half-an-hour before Ken was due to pick her up, so why not? Besides, Mac was engaging company.

Mac handed her a small glass of water and the spatula. "If the bacon fat catches fire, just douse it. I'll be right back."

True to his word, he returned a moment later with a mint-green concoction that looked inviting. Kelly turned over his cooking utensils and accepted the drink gratefully. It was as good as it looked.

"Umm!" she remarked, licking her upper lip where the frosty liquid stuck to it. "Are you good at everything you do?"

His eyes danced as they swept over her and then rested on hers. "I do my darnedest," he answered suggestively.

"You're home early," she said, glancing at her

watch nervously, under his discomforting appraisal, in an attempt to divert the undertone of the conversation she had unwittingly started.

He shrugged, his eyes still alight with humor. "You know what they say about all work and no play." Kelly was relieved when he began to concentrate on the shrimp he was turning. "So, tonight's the team's big night out, eh?"

"What? Oh," Kelly chuckled as she recalled the girls telling him about Susie's party. "Yes, it is. You know, I'm not sure I want to go through all this when I get married. I'm just the maid of honor and to tell the truth, I am exhausted from all this pre-wedding chaos. What about you? I mean, what big plans do you have for tonight?" she added quickly, seeing one dark brow raise quizzically.

"I am going to enjoy these shrimp and sit back and watch a movie on the VCR. Then, I am going to hit the sack early for a change so I can rest up for the big gala tomorrow."

"You have been working a lot," Kelly gave him sympathetically.

"Okay, this one is ready for sampling," he announced, sliding one of the jumbo shrimp off the skewer to a paper plate. "Now . . ." He looked at Kelly and shook his head in disapproval. "We can't have you ruining that outfit." After a quick search, he seized a tea towel and wrapped it about her neck.

"You're crazy," Kelly laughed, raising her hands to the back of her head to tie it tighter.

"I've been accused of worse!" He winked impishly, as he cut the shrimp into bite-sized portions. "Now, you should get your fingers all greasy and covered with the sauce, but since you are going out, I'll do the honors."

To her surprise, he picked up a piece and shoved it in her mouth, smearing sauce on her face in the process. Kelly chewed the morsel thoughtfully before nodding, her eyes sparkling in approval.

"Delicious!"

"Now, if you were not my employee, I could think of a much better way to take care of that sauce, but since we are strictly business . . ." he picked up a corner of the towel and wiped her mouth daintily, "we'll do things conventionally."

"You're awful!" Kelly chastised good-naturedly, her face pinkening. "But you're a good barbecuer!"

She reached behind her to take away the towel, but the clasp of her necklace was caught in the terry cloth. She frowned as she tried to disengage it, but it would not give.

"Here, let me."

Mac stood in front of her and leaned over to assist. He parted her hair to either side of the tangle, his fingers touching her neck and sending shivers up her spine. Her face was a breath away from the dark curls on his chest where his cotton shirt had been carelessly left open. She fought the overwhelming urge to nuzzle it, forcing her breath out determinedly.

This attraction she felt for this man was unsettling, to say the least. Was this what was lacking in her relationship with Ken, she wondered. Was this the reason for her reluctance to set a wedding date . . . and his? She enjoyed Ken's kisses. She enjoyed his caresses, but they did not affect her like the simple contact she was experiencing now.

"That's got it!" Mac announced, drawing the towel off her shoulders, which were left bare by the halter top of her jumpsuit. "Just hold still till I re-fasten your necklace."

Kelly obeyed mutely, her thoughts racing in confusion. When he tossed the towel aside, one hand still holding her necklace in place, and leaned over her once more, her cheek brushed his chest, the crisp hair tickling it. Kelly jerked involuntarily, placing a distance between her face and the inviting pillow of muscle. If Mac noticed her reaction, he did not show it.

"There! You're all set . . . and just in time," he added wryly as a horn beeped in the parking lot.

Kelly jumped to her feet, wondering how long Ken had been there. Of course, nothing had happened, an internal voice began in defense of the rising warmth of her skin.

"Thank you for the sample and the drink!" she

called, retreating down the steps with her clutch shoved under her arm.

"Enjoy yourself, Ace!"

Kelly did not acknowledge Mac's reference to the nickname the girls had given her. Her eyes were on the brooding face of her fiance. Ken always came to the door to pick her up, so she knew he had seen enough to fuel his dislike for Mac that much more, even though it was totally innocent.

"Hi!" she greeted brightly through the window of the sedan before opening the door and getting inside. "I was just trying some of Mac's barbe-cued shrimp. I've got to get his recipe."

"So do I, it seems."

Kelly assumed a puzzled look as she faced the man beside her and then shrugged his caustic comment away. "My aren't you handsome!" she said, valiantly trying to restore his good humor. "If some girl comes out of a cake tonight at that bach-elor party, you tell her your spoken for."

"You might keep that same advice in mind for yourself, Kelly," he replied acidly, accelerating the car so suddenly that her head was thrown against the headrest.

"I doubt we'll have a guy coming out of a cake," she countered, pretending his comment went over her head.

"You know damned well what I mean." He shot a barbed look across the seat at her. Sud-denly, he laughed to himself bitterly. "Or maybe you don't. As hip as you are with your damned flying, you are plain stupid when it comes to men. He's setting you up for the kill. Before you know it, you'll be in his bed, just like dozens before you."

"I'm touched by your faith in me, Ken," Kelly said, her eyes accusing and hurt at the same time.

His muffled curse set the tone for the evening. He remained sullen in spite of Kelly's buoyant attempts to cheer him. The fun and teasing at the wedding rehearsal helped Kelly maintain her gay demeanor. It was her best friend's night and she was determined not to let Ken ruin everything with his sour disposition. But the teases about Kelly and Ken making it a double wedding only worsened the tension between them.

When the rehearsal and dinner were over, Kelly felt as if she had been released from confinement. But it wasn't until the girls reached the supper club where Kaye had made reservations that the strain began to show. The ladies and gents had parted company with friendly warnings to behave themselves, but Ken's was serious. Kelly had been silent the whole way over to the club in Spike's van, a distinct contrast to the others who were already having a good time enhanced by the cocktails at the dinner.

"Okay, Ace, what's the problem with you and Kennie?" Spike demanded, a strong hand clasping Kelly's shoulder in comfort.

Kelly sighed heavily and leaned on the table

with folded arms. "He thinks there is something going on between Mac Mackenzie and me . . . and there isn't."

"God, that would depress me, too!" Kaye exclaimed in mock dismay, deliberately taking the wrong meaning. "It does, as a matter of fact. Waiter, two godmothers on the rocks," she called out to the god-like young bodybuilder who wore tight black pants, his body bare from the waist up with the exception of a black bow tie over a starched white collar.

"What's a godmother?" Kelly asked dubiously.

"A non-depressant," Kaye answered, watching the sinewy back of the retreating waiter.

"There aren't any lady waitresses in here!" Susie confided to Kelly, making her immediately forget her problems with Ken as she recalled the purpose of the evening. "It looks like one of those playgirl clubs I've read about."

Pretending to check out her friend's observation, Kelly nodded in feigned innocence. "There's mostly just women customers, too."

"My God, this is paradise!" Kaye declared, hungrily watching another waiter pass by their table. "If these are the waiters, I can't wait for the show!"

"You're depraved, woman!" Spike teased, as a drum roll brought spotlights to a small stage that jutted out to divide the room into two sections.

"What's the name of the show, Kaye?" Susie

asked in a raised voice to be heard over the loud music that ensued.

"You'll see, sweetie! It's recommended for all young ladies about to get married. I think I read about it in one of those wedding books!" she added impishly.

"I think I'm being had," Susie groaned suspiciously.

Kelly, unable to contain her amusement any longer, burst out laughing as a handsome blonde cowboy came out on the stage. He proceeded to unfurl a lariat from his belt and perform rope tricks that brought applause from the audience, all the while moving his lithe form to the music. She had just decided it wasn't going to be as rough as she thought, when a matronly woman on the other side of the stage stood up and shouted.

"Let's see what else you got, Tex!"

"First, I need a partner. Any volunteers?" the cowboy called out to the cheering audience.

The crowd erupted with waving hands and offers.

The cowboy shook his head. "So many pretty fillies, I just can't choose. I guess I'll have to let my rope pick one out. Just keep your hands down ladies," he instructed as he strolled around the stage eyeing the crowd, his lariat whirling above his head.

Kelly saw the rope lash out and gasped as it dropped over Kaye.

"Holy cow! The poor soul won't have a stitch

left when she's done with him!" Spike giggled, as Kaye eagerly climbed up on the stage.

If the cowpoke expected a timid participant, he received the shock of his life. Kaye fell right into the music and carried the routine out to its end. When the music stopped, Susie was peeking through her fingers as Kaye stepped down off the stage with his bandana tied around her neck. The dancer left the stage carrying all his clothes with the exception of a pair of bikini briefs and his ten-gallon hat.

"I'm going to kill you, Kaye Phippin!" the bride-to-be threatened as the woman took her seat. "If Doug hears we came here, he'll have a fit!"

"What's good for the goose is good for the gander!" Kaye quoted glibly.

The music stepped up again and a group of dancers came out in disco clothing. When they were reduced to briefs and ties, they wandered through the audience, stopping to take tips. Kelly sat between the table and the wall, protected, but Susie was at the end of the table. One of the well-developed, shining bodies swung her chair around and proceeded to go into a series of gyrations in front of her that had her shrieking in embarrassment and amusement at the same time.

Kelly turned away and finished her second god-mother, laughing sympathetically. Susie would be the first beet-red bride in history because Kelly was certain her shy friend's color would never return to normal. As if testing, she touched her hand to her own cheek to find it more than warm to the touch and allowed that she might be the first beet-red maid of honor.

The evening soon became a blur. Ken the furthest thought from her mind, Kelly joked and carried on with her friends until the lights were turned up to indicate it was time to go home. Susie was now long past embarrassment and accepted the congratulatory kisses on the cheek from the young male dancers as their group walked out the door. Kaye had passed out all the cards she had, and Spike brought up the rear, tucking away a single phone number of her own unobtrusively. She grinned mischievously as she realized Kelly had seen her.

Spike, who had been drinking lemon tonic the better part of the evening, drove the others home. Kelly was the first to be dropped off. As she struggled on wobbly heels up the walk, the girls tooted the horn, singing in dissonant chorus out the windows the words to an old song about wedding bells breaking up the old gang before driving off. Still humming the tune, Kelly began to search through her clutch for her key, her coordination leaving much to be desired. A grin spread on her face as she grasped it and tried to get it into the lock. The end hit the metal and the key clattered to the deck.

"Oh, no!" With a half-laugh and half-moan, Kelly dropped to her knees unceremoniously to feel about for the runaway key.

When she could not find it, she realized it must have fallen through the decking. Upon crawling to the edge, she lowered her top half over the side and tried to peer under the patio, hoping that the bright moon overhead would shed enough light through the cracks to permit her to see her key. Her balance precarious at best, she felt herself sliding forward into the shrubs planted in front of the stoop and cried out in alarm.

"Whoa, Ace!" Strong hands encircled her waist, halting her fall and hauled her back onto the deck, her head bumping the lower rail as she slid beneath it.

"Ow!" she protested, her hand going to the wound as she rolled over to see her rescuer. "Oh, hi, Mac!"

"Aren't we though!" he remarked with wry amusement, holding out his hand to help her up. "What were you doing?"

"Trying to get in the house."

The sudden movement of his pulling her up made her dizzy. He caught her as she swayed forward on the high heels.

"Most people use the door."

Kelly laughed softly, burying her face in the hair of his chest. "I dropped my key, silly." She lifted her face to meet his, inadvertently rubbing her nose where the crisp dark curls had tickled it. "It's under there," she said, pointing down. "Do you have a flashlight?"

Mac's arms tightened about her as her heel

buckled under her. "I tell you what. You come on inside my place and get out of those shoes before you fall off and hurt yourself. I'll fix you some coffee and breakfast and then we'll look for your key."

"Sounds goo . . . what are you doing?" Kelly exclaimed as her legs were swept out from under her. Instinctively, she wrapped her arms about his neck.

"That's the idea, Ace," he coaxed, brushing the top of her head with his lips as he carried her into his apartment.

He lowered her gently onto the sofa and took off her shoes, before going into the kitchen to carry out his promise. Kelly leaned on the arm of the sofa, unaware of the sultry pose she had assumed, one long leg drawn up over the other outstretched one, her upper torso twisted to show her feminine curves to their fullest advantage.

"I guess I don't have to ask you if you had a good time," Mac teased, taking some bacon and eggs from the refrigerator.

"I never saw anything like it! They were all but naked. But I guess some of the guys on the beach don't wear much more than that. But then I pretended I saw those shows everyday because if they thought I didn't . . . hadn't," she corrected herself with a slight frown at her confusing words, "they would have gotten me up there like they did Susie. I stayed behind at the table. You wouldn't believe what they did!"

Kelly, totally uninhibited and wide-eyed, proceeded to tell him, stopping at intervals for his appropriately impressed comments, given in barely suppressed amusement that Kelly missed. When her chatter finally wound down and her eyelids grew heavy, she became aware of a gentle shaking of her shoulders and blinked up at the face above hers in bewilderment.

"Time to eat, you wicked little imp."

Kelly placed her hand over her mouth and yawned as he dragged her to her feet and held her against him. "I'm not hungry."

She laid her cheek against his chest and closed her eyes, her arms going about his waist seeking the warmth and comfort of his body instinctively. His moaned oath did not register and she was barely aware that he had gathered her totally in his arms. She seemed to be floating on air, curled against him, her head nestled in the hollow of his pulsing throat. Then there was a distant creak as a mattress gave under their weight before all sense of her surroundings faded in the darkness of sound sleep.

SIX

Her throat was dry. Her tongue felt like a large cotton ball stuck to the roof of her mouth. Kelly's lips moved tentatively, tasting the acrid coating on her tongue and wrinkling her nose in distaste. Surely, she never drank anything that was so foul! Water, the hazy thought straggled to the forefront of her sleep.

The long lashes that lay fanned on her cheeks in repose, rose in a blinking fashion until her eyes stared at her strange surroundings in bewilderment. Where on earth was she? She lifted her head and groaned as a pain erupted through her sleepy stupor. The foam pillow might as well have been concrete for all the comfort it offered. The agony being as intense lying still as moving, Kelly forced herself up to her knees and surveyed the room where she had slept through heavy-lidded eyes.

It was a masculine room, decorated in bold plaid drapes that shut out most of the offending sunlight. A matching bedspread lay at the foot of the king-size bed she knelt on. She lifted the edge of the sheet, idly noting that they matched also. The layout being oddly familiar, she found her way to the tiled bathroom and helped herself to several cups full of water, before focusing on the disheveled girl in the mirror.

The golden hair she had so carefully styled the night before was in a ridiculous tumble of curls. Tiny lines of red streaked the white around her dull blue eyes. Her makeup was smudged, making her look like she had been in a fight and lost. Spying a neatly folded navy washcloth, she wet it and applied it to her face. Whatever had happened to her, she couldn't stay like this, wherever she was. But it hurt her mind too much to concern herself with that at the moment.

The cold water refreshed her. Perhaps a shower would at least help her through the crisis of this certain terminal illness. She glanced down and began to unbutton the oversized pajama shirt when her fingers froze. Mac Mackenzie had had on pants just like this last night! Kelly leaned forward and gripped the edge of the sink miserably. Where were her clothes? What had they done? She winced at the flood of questions as she made her way cautiously into the living area.

It appeared that she was alone in the apartment. In dreadful apprehension, she glanced around, the events of the previous night coming back to her. She recalled Mac helping her into his apartment and cooking in the kitchen. Her face turned scarlet as she remembered her colorful description of the all-male review. Frowning in frustration as her memory came to a standstill, she wandered over to the kitchen counter where a sandwich lay wrapped in foil beside a note with two aspirin and her key on it. Her hands trembled slightly as she picked up the note and read it.

"Dear drinking buddy," it began, "I recommend you take these, drink the coffee that's on the warmer, and eat the sandwich. If you're not better by then, try the Bloody Mary in the refrigerator. Then use the key. See you at the wedding." It was signed, "Mac."

Kelly obeyed his instructions to the letter, with the exception of the Bloody Mary. She vowed never to let alcohol cross her lips again as she chewed softly to avoid aggravating the throbbing that had dulled to a steady ache in her head. Her eyes wandered about the room idly, falling on the sofa where a pillow and rumpled blanket lay. The matching bottoms to her pajama top were balled up at the foot of the makeshift bed.

"Oh!" she sighed in relief, blessing Mac Mackenzie for being a gentleman.

A smug smile tugged at the corners of her mouth as she thought of Ken's unjust accusation. She didn't dare point out how gallant her neighbor had been, though. As unreasonable as Ken had become, she would never convince him that nothing had happened. Although Mac had undressed her, she frowned, glancing down at her . . . his shirt and gaining color in her cheeks.

Convinced that she was going to live, Kelly began to search for her jumpsuit, which she discovered under the covers rammed down at the foot of the king-size bed. Suddenly, she wanted to be out of there before Mac came home. She was not prepared to face anyone, but especially him, after having made such an utter fool of herself. Again, she added remorsefully.

She covered her eyes to protect them from the assault of the sun as she scampered across the deck to her own apartment and let herself in, grateful that she had seen no one walking about. The phone rang as she tossed her heels in the closet and she answered it. It was Sue in a panic because she didn't have something old. Kelly thought for a moment, enduring the pain it cost.

"I have a cameo ring that belonged to my grandmother somewhere. I'll let you use that," she promised. "It'll look lovely with your gown . . . very Victorian. See you in a couple of hours."

Kelly glared at the clock that seemed to step up its timekeeping to make her rush as she dressed for the wedding. By the time she showered and donned the tea-length, strapless gown Susie had chosen for her, Mac's prescription had done the trick. She applied just the slightest amount of blush to match the mauve taffeta of her dress before going out to her old thunderbird to drive to the church.

The wedding was a traditional affair, beautiful in its simplicity. Doug was white under his tan as he made his vows, perspiration beading on his forehead, while Susie went through the motions like an automaton, cool and mechanical. It wasn't until everyone arrived at the club for the reception that things seemed to relax.

A band played a variety of music to suit the different ages of the guests. Kelly stood next to Susie in the receiving line while countless introductions were made. After a while, her smile became fixed, and she felt like talking through her teeth, but resisted the temptation.

"I see you survived last night's ordeal rather well, at least by all appearances," Mac Mackenzie added with a surreptitious wink as he took her hand between his.

Kelly's pasted-on smile widened sheepishly.

"Did we wake you up when we dropped Kelly off, Mr. Mackenzie?" Susie asked apologetically. It had taken two doses of painkiller before the bride was ready to face the wedding, she'd confessed to Kelly earlier. It seemed the girls had outpartied the guys.

"Just our complex," Mac assured her mischievously. "I don't think the one on the next block heard you."

Susie gave a low moan of apology, but cut it short as she realized he was teasing. Mac moved on down the line, congratulating the groom. The best man ignored his offered hand and Kelly's mouth set firmly in a line, her smile abandoned. Ken had been barely civil throughout the afternoon, what little chance she'd had to see him. She had hoped a night out with the boys would improve his humor.

When the line finally broke up, Kelly took her place at the head table next to the bride for the formal dinner that followed. Spike and Kaye were to her right, both pretty in ecru dresses styled like Kelly's with mauve trim, while Ken and the other ushers sat on the left of the now-smiling groom. After a delicious prime rib with asparagus hollandaise and stuffed potatoes, Ken made an appropriate toast and the dancing began. According to tradition, Susie and Doug led the dancing, followed by Kelly and Ken and so forth, until all the wedding party were on the dance floor.

As Ken held her stiffly in his arms, Kelly looked up at him in exasperation. "Are you going to permanently assume this sour disposition or dispense with it and have fun?"

His brown eyes bore into hers heatedly. "Where were you all of last night?"

"Out with the girls, why?"

"At three, four, five, six, seven . . . until noon?" he challenged, his arms tightening painfully about her. At her astounded silence, he went on. "I called your place every hour on the hour,

Kelly, to make sure you got home alright. Spike told me she dropped you off at three.''

"You are hurting me, Kenneth Hudson, and I don't like being interrogated like some prisoner of war. Now, let me go!'' she demanded, pushing against his chest angrily. "This is a special day for our best friends. The least you can do is be civil. Then tomorrow, you can act any damned way you please,'' she hissed under her breath.

She whirled away from him and made a straight line toward the table where Dan Mooney sat. Her legs were shaking when she dropped down in a vacant chair beside him and placed her arm around his shoulder in a brief hug.

"Trouble?'' he asked perceptively, seeing through her forced smile.

"I don't know what has gotten into Ken lately. He is unreasonably resentful of Mac. He says Mac is an opportunist who takes what he wants regardless of anyone's feelings, and he thinks Mac is after me. God, nothing could be further from the truth!''

"Which one?'' her adopted uncle teased, pinching the end of her upturned nose.

"Both,'' Kelly admitted sullenly.

"He'll probably tell you that Mac got his start in this business by marrying into it, too. That's been a pretty popular rumor. Men like Mackenzie generate lots of speculation as to the reason for their success, Kelly . . . usually by people who haven't made it themselves. They fail to see his industriousness and shrewdness because they're too jealous to recognize it.''

"But Ken has no reason to be jealous. He . . . he's just as good-looking and certainly has potential. He just hasn't reached the goals he's set for himself," Kelly objected, defending her fiance as much to herself as to Uncle Dan.

Uncle Dan took a sip of the champagne punch. "He's no Mac Mackenzie."

"Uncle Dan, who's side are you on?" Her eyes implored him to help her.

"Yours," he confided with a wink. "Always yours, Kelly. Remember that when I'm gone."

"Don't talk like that!" she chided, hugging him again. "You're the only man I can trust. What would I do without you?"

"I think you're being paged," he informed her, nodding to where a group of her friends were motioning for her to join them.

"All single ladies, please gather in the center of the dance floor!"

Her whole life was starting to come apart at the seams and she had these tedious little games to play out, she thought, as she left Uncle Dan to join the group of giggling girls aspiring to catch the bridal bouquet.

"Alright now. You're engaged and Kaye has been married once already, so you guys block for me while I catch it," Spike planned as Kelly joined them.

Kelly grinned at her friend's enthusiasm and

agreed, but when Susie tossed the bouquet on the count of three, it landed squarely in her hands.

"It's a conspiracy between blondes!" Spike cried out in mock indignation. "Even the girl on the cake is a blonde!"

Kelly laughed. "Here, Spike, it's all yours."

"No, I don't want it secondhand!" her brown-haired teammate declined, overly incredulous that she should suggest such a thing. "But at your wedding, you get a good look at where I am and throw it in my direction, okay?"

"Okay."

Kelly moved with the group out of the way for the groom to toss the garter Susan had worn, a pretty blue satin one with white lace and a tiny seed pearl heart decorating it. She hardly saw who caught it, her mind on Ken as she absently depetaled a daisy. She had seen a side of him that was foreign to her and she didn't like it.

"Well go on, Kelly. You won him fair and square!"

Spike interrupted her reverie by shoving her out onto the dance floor where Mac Mackenzie waited, the garter hanging on his finger as he raised it to show her. Automatically, Kelly's eyes sought out Ken in time to see his mouth tighten in a grim line before he stepped through the door. She didn't think matters could get any worse, but the cheers egging Mac to raise the garter that he placed on her leg higher and higher seemed to emphasize her trouble.

"It seems fate has destined us to be together," Mac jested, taking her into his arms and swinging her around in time to the music of their dance. "I am making an exception for you, you know," he whispered, his eyes traveling over her head to the closing door Ken Hudson had just disappeared through.

"Oh?" Kelly asked morosely, unconsciously pressing closer for comfort.

"I don't usually hold my pilots like this when I dance with them."

Her shoulders shook as she chuckled in spite of her distress. Mac lifted her chin so that he could see her face.

"Now, that's much better. For a moment you looked as though you were walking into an execution instead of my arms."

Unlike Ken, Mac held her firmly, but moved in a relaxed manner. He was an excellent dancer, using pressure at the small of her back to guide her smoothly about the floor. His aftershave was as deeply virile and masculine as the wearer. Kelly felt her pulse step up its pace at the decidedly arousing contact with the lean body that strained the shoulders of his tailored jacket.

"Do you usually undress your pilots and put them to bed when they've had enough to drink to make a complete fool of themselves?" Kelly wondered aloud, amazed at how easy it was to forget Ken in Mac's arms.

"I've put buddies to bed on more than one

occasion . . . and have had to be put down a time or two myself,'' he admitted, his eyes warming her blood as they looked into her soul.

Could he possibly know how she felt, she thought breathlessly, glancing away to protect her innermost feelings. No, he was just carrying on a cheery conversation. He caught a silly garter and she caught the bouquet. If not for that, he probably wouldn't have danced with her at all. Especially with Ken breathing down his neck. As their employer, Mac did not need that kind of complication in his ranks.

''But you take the prize for being the best looking of the bunch.''

''Thanks,'' Kelly answered with a sarcastic grin as the dance came to an end. ''And thanks for the exception.''

''My pleasure, Ace.''

Kelly walked away feeling more dejected than ever. Ken was no where to be seen in the corridor. A quick check in the parking lot revealed his sedan was not parked where Kelly had seen it as they entered the club. He was really outdoing himself tonight, she thought bitterly, as she went back inside to join the others.

After the bride and groom said their good-bys and left in a hilariously decorated car, she helped Susie's mom and dad load the presents in their station wagon and then left herself. As she pulled into the parking lot in front of her apartment, she noticed a light on by the television. Although

Kelly didn't recall leaving one on, she didn't think much of it until she found the door unlocked.

"Mrs. Brooks?" she called out, hesitating at the entrance suspiciously.

"It's only me, Kelly."

Ken stepped out from behind the kitchen counter, a drink in his hand. With a sigh of relief, Kelly entered and closed the screen behind her, leaving the heavy glass door open to permit the cool breeze off the water to blow in. He had discarded his tuxedo jacket on the sofa along with the tie. The ruffled front of his shirt had been unbuttoned casually at the neck.

It was odd, Kelly thought as he walked over to her, that at first she had mistaken Mac for Ken. Their only similarity was dark hair and both were tall, although, side by side, Mac was the taller of the two. Ken's features were softer, prettily handsome, where Mac's were ruggedly so. And of course, while Ken's eyes were a warm brown, Mac's were that haunting, elusive grey.

"Did I tell you you were beautiful this afternoon?" he asked, cupping his hand under her chin.

"No. That would have been a compliment and you were more inclined toward interrogation," she answered coolly.

The hand moved along the tapered line of her cheeks in a caress. His voice trembled slightly as he spoke. "I have never been able to hold you, Kelly. I've never felt like you were really mine."

"Ken, I have never been out with anyone since I accepted this ring. I did not take that commitment lightly," she objected stubbornly.

The way his lip curled sent a shiver of apprehension down her spine. "A ring?" he sneered contemptuously. "It's a worthless piece of jewelry. You've never made the commitment I need."

His fingers slipped around her face to lock in her hair, drawing her head back. There was something in his eyes that frightened her more than the painful tug of her hair. An arm snaked around her waist, crushing her against him. His liquored breath assaulted her nostrils as he spoke, his face inches from her own.

"You were with him last night." It was not a question, but a statement of fact. "I saw you coming out of his apartment shortly after noon."

"You were watching me!" Kelly gasped in incredulous indignation.

"I used to think you were adorably naive," he laughed acidly. "Now I know you were a consummate actress, my sweet little Kelly."

"I dropped my key through the deck and slept in Mac's apartment . . . alone," she blurted out furiously, emphasizing the last word. "He slept on the sofa like a gentleman."

"Liar!"

His mouth came down on hers, crushing her lips painfully against her teeth as she struggled in his vise-like grasp. She twisted in his embrace and shoved her elbow against his throat desperately.

"No!" she cried out, swinging her hand and slapping his face sharply as he backed away in surprise. "How dare you!" She pushed him again, forcing him back a few more steps. "I don't like being manhandled, threatened, accused of infidelity, and being called a liar." Kelly jerked the diamond off her finger. "If this is worthless, then I don't want it. And I don't want you! Get out of here and don't you ever come back!" She choked in anger. "Out!" she demanded, snatching up his jacket and shoving it at him.

"Kelly . . ."

"Damn you, I'll call the police if you're not through that door by the count of three!"

As his headlights turned toward the road and the sedan merged in with the other night traffic, Kelly began to shake. If she hadn't taken the offensive . . . A shudder of revulsion made her grasp her arms, rubbing them as if to erase his touch. She went over to the kitchen counter where the bottle of bourbon he had helped himself to sat and poured a stiff drink. It burned as she drank it straight down, forgetting her vow of that morning. My God, how could she have ever thought she loved that man, she wondered, refilling her glass with trembling hands.

She drew in a shaky breath. The breeze had stilled and suddenly she felt as if she would suffocate in the confines of the room. Wiping perspiration from her brow with the clammy palm of her hand, she went outside and sought the privacy of the pool area. Without regard for her dress, she gave into the impulse to dive in the cool water. Ignoring the hampering swirls of taffeta about her legs, she began to swim laps in long, hard strokes, venting her rage and frustration until her lungs felt as though they would burst from the exertion.

"Are you alright?"

Startled, Kelly looked up from the concrete where she had rested her head on her arms to see Mac Mackenzie kneeling in front of her.

"Fine." Her voice wavered with emotion.

Mac's face was grim as he studied her. "I couldn't help but overhear. When I heard that splash, I didn't know what you were up to so . . ."

"I'm not suicidal," she assured him sarcastically. "I just came to my senses before it was too late." She sniffed and brushed her naturally curly hair out of her face, only to have it fall back rebelliously. "I never dreamed he could be such a jerk!"

Mac took her wrists and effortlessly pulled her out of the water. "How about if we talk about it on dry land?" He grabbed a section of her dripping skirt and wrung it out, proceeding around its full circumference until it ceased to trail water. "Now, maybe you won't make too much of a mess," he teased, putting his arm around her and guiding her back to the building.

It seemed natural for him to take her in her bedroom and unfasten her dress. It fell in a wet heap at her feet, which he lifted her out of. With a smoothness derived from experience, he relieved her of her panty hose. As she sat on the edge of the bed, clad only in her thin lace bra and panties, the air-conditioning he'd turned on before closing the sliding door to her apartment blew directly on her from the overhead vent and she shivered.

"Come here, Kelly."

It was a gentle command that she obeyed willingly, seeking the warmth of his arms. Yet, his embrace was far from comforting. The warmth surpassed comfort and spread through her like a brush fire. Her skin burned where his hands roamed over the soft and supple curves of her body. Her breasts rose and fell against his chest with her uneven breaths. At his soft moan, her lips moved of their own accord to his neck while her fingers did away with the last buttons of his shirt. She circled his lean waist with her arms, seeking his flesh with her own.

"Kelly." Her name sounded like a caress.

She raised her heated gaze to meet his own hungry one. Her lips parted under the sensuous assault of his mouth. The searing exploration of his tongue took her breath, nearly rendering her unconscious with a bombardment of sensations running riot through her body. Never had she been kissed so completely before, nor had she known such desperation in her response.

"Mac!" she cried, reaching for sanity against the tide of desire, but his name became a moaned plea for more.

She slowly eased back on the bed, dragging him with her in an instinctive seduction, the knowledge of which he had somehow managed to reveal to her through the erotic stimulation he tortured her with. An aching need that consumed her drove her hips against his as he weighted them back to the mattress, his own need now evident to her through the lightweight material of his trousers. She became ignited by it. Her writhing and exploring touch, which managed to slip over the rippling flesh of his back under his shirt, made him gasp and shudder so violently that he shook her as well.

There was an expression of shock on his face as she reached up and clasped it between her hands. "Love me, Mac, please. Forget I'm your pilot." .

He stared at her, his face a mirror of unprecedented confusion. Suddenly, he cursed under his breath and rolled away. His leaving exposed her to the cool air that seemed to match the chill of his rejection. The harsh slap of reality struck her dumb as shame colored her crimson from head to foot. Crossing her arms in front of herself in belated modesty, Kelly jumped up and ran into the bathroom, slamming the door behind her. Her fingers fumbled with the lock as she heard him call her name and get up to follow.

"Kelly!"

"I'm going to take a bath and then go to bed. Please don't be here when I come out, Mac," she pleaded, her voice choked with tears. What in heaven's name had come over her, she wondered in mortification.

"Kelly, let me in."

"Go away, Mac Mackenzie! Just go away!" Alone. That's what she had to be. She needed to collect herself.

"You don't understand . . ."

"Go away!"

She waited, her breath frozen, until she heard the grating slide of the patio door before venturing out of her sanctuary. Hurriedly, she ran to lock it and draw the drapes. After the lights were out, she threw herself across the bed in the lonely darkness and gave into the sobs that tore at her wretchedly until her ragged breaths became soft whimpers in a restless sleep.

SEVEN

Tulum. Kelly scanned her charts in the office provided for the Custom Aero pilots, mapping out the course she would be taking to the remote Mexican city on the Yucatan peninsula. She would have to fly to Merida first and check in with the authorities before continuing on to the coastal city. She also had to make sure she had all the documents needed to fly into Mexico without a hassle—passport, pilot's license, medical certificate, and personal radio license. In addition, for her plane she would need the registration, an air-worthiness certificate, a flight manual, a radio station license, and Mexican liability insurance.

She'd better call Mac's secretary and remind her to make sure the company had taken care of that little item, she thought, putting down her pencil and taking up the phone. Although Kelly had no intention of having any sort of accident, it was not worth the risk of arrest and possible imprisonment.

The better part of the week she had been idle, the other corporate pilot taking most of the flights. Mac had had her fly him to Dallas and leave him there. He had also seen that the flight she was originally scheduled for to take Ken back to St. Louis had been turned over to the other pilot, at least that's what his secretary told her on the sly in the cafeteria.

Kelly appreciated that thoughtful gesture. The last person she wanted to shuttle around was Ken Hudson, at least for the time being. He'd sent a bouquet of roses to the hangar before she left to take Mac to Dallas with a note that read simply, "I'm sorry." She had taken them over to the trash barrel at the edge of the strip and dumped them unceremoniously, vase and all. She had meant what she said to Ken. It was over.

As for Mac, there was little left to think about there. On the few times they happened to run into each other, she was grateful that he acted as if nothing had happened between them the night of the wedding. When he wasn't in Dallas, he was at the office until late, so she had little opportunity to see him. And that was just as well, she consoled herself, still horrified at her brazen behavior. Congenial distance was the answer. Under the circumstances, her employer was more than fair.

News about her break with Ken had spread fast. She had already been asked out for the weekend, but this sudden trip to Mexico interfered with that. She hadn't really wanted to go out anyway. Her experiences with men of late had not been the most successful and she felt she needed time to sort things out.

"Hi, Midge? This is Kelly. Did you make the arrangements for our insurance?"

"Sure did. I have all the documents in the brief-case Mac asked me to put together," the cheery voice on the other end of the line assured her. "Oh, he telephoned from Dallas. He's flying himself in Saturday. He asked me to tell you to pack light cotton clothing and a few nice outfits for going out."

"He's entertaining the client, not me," Kelly replied in surprise.

She had planned, however, on taking some nicer things. Since she would be spending a week so close to Cancun and Cozumel, she thought she'd venture over to the popular resorts on her own. The travel agency said it was about a five-to six-hour boat ride from the Quintana Roo mainland. She almost felt guilty about enjoying a mini, paid vacation in Mexico when she knew how badly the girls wanted to go.

"I'm just repeating the boss's orders," Midge laughed. "But I wish I'd taken up flying," she added with a twinge of jealousy. "Imagine, getting paid to lie on a beach with those dark Mexican men all around."

"I'll send you a postcard," Kelly teased. "Talk to you later. I'll be set for take off Monday morning unless I hear differently."

There were so many things to do before Monday morning that when it arrived, Kelly's head was spinning. Her luggage was stowed in the rear, she thought, checking that item off her memory jogger list. She'd prepared a written flight plan to present to the Mexican authorities at the entry airport and left copies with the Custom Aero tower. Check. She made sure Mickey put in a fuel strainer, since Mexican aviation fuel was often stored above ground, allowing moisture to dilute it. She didn't need an engine stall over the blue waters of the Gulf on the return trip. And she had oxygen, just in case, a survival kit, tie-down equipment, and aeronautical charts of the Yucatan and the area between the peninsula and Corpus Christi.

When she made a smooth takeoff and bade the guys at the Tower a smug farewell, she had the nagging feeling that she had forgotten something, but every item on her list had a check by it. It was a clear day, warm and humid. For her own pleasure, she dropped to a lower altitude to look at the shimmering and seemingly endless expanse of water. Although Mac was in the passenger section working on a set of prints, she felt as though she were alone in flight and it made her spirits soar.

As soon as she was in range, she began radio contact with the Mexican authorities, aware that they preferred it that way. There were so many horror stories of forced landings, confiscations of planes, and innocent pilots being arrested for some inadvertant oversight in the Mexican red-tape requirements, that Kelly was, perhaps, a bit over-cautious. One of her friends had once teased that flying to Mexico was a great experience as long as one didn't land.

Upon landing in Merida, Kelly thought she would suffocate. The air-conditioning in the terminal was out of service. She stood beside Mac, permitting him to handle the authorities with his fluent Spanish while she produced all the certificates and papers she had brought along and let them sort them out. Two hours later, with all their documents in order and ninety-day visitors' cards, they were refueled and took off for Tulum.

The red tape at the small Tulum airstrip took even longer, to her surprise. Kelly browsed through assorted brochures of places to visit while Mac handled everything. She smiled as she recognized a picture of a large grey fist of rock that rose from the azure waters of the sea that was the ruins of the Mayan civilization called the Castillo. She had had the same view as she had circled the city for a landing.

"Kelly, would you come put your John Henry where the X's are and we'll be on our way," Mac requested, distracting her from her sightseeing plans.

Mac stood over a desk where a white-suited man with typical, dark Mexican coloring flashed a broad smile at her. Perspiration beaded Mac's forehead and the light blue shirt he wore was splotched with it as well, his jacket having been shed on the plane. Kelly took the pen he handed her and signed where he indicated, not bothering to decipher the Spanish words. Mac had successfully seen them through the port of entry and she trusted him completely to handle the paperwork. Otherwise, they would be there another hour while she painstakingly looked up the words she needed in her dictionary. She couldn't believe the amount of paperwork necessary for a simple week's stay.

"Congratulations, senora. It is my hope that you enjoy your stay at the Villa Bianca."

Kelly raised her eyebrows in puzzlement and looked at Mac.

"Our client's villa . . . We'll be staying there," he explained, placing his hand at the small of her back where her jumpsuit clung damply.

"Shouldn't I stay at a hotel since . . ."

"It's all arranged," Mac cut her off with a grin. "Stop worrying."

She did just that. Standing at the rail of the small motor launch that Mac engaged to take them to the villa, his having explained that the trip through the jungle roads would take much longer and be much more uncomfortable, she was cool for the first time that day. The air that rushed through her hair made a curling tumble of the sleek style she had blown-dry that morning and dried out her flightsuit. The first thing she would do upon arrival was try one of the beautiful beaches they were passing, she mused quietly.

"Look there," Mac instructed, his words so close to her ear that she started.

Stiffening at his proximity and the bronzed arms that held the rail on either side of her, she followed his gaze over the side. The boat had slowed so she could see a breathtaking display of color beneath the clear surface. A lace wall of coral almost within reach looked like blistered mountains and caverns where a vast and odd variety of fish fed and made their home. Fleeting lights reflected as the fish, some fat and vulgar, scampered in and about the grottos to make outraged faces at the boat skimming over them, while others glided sleek and silvery with eager, puckered mouths to enjoy Neptune's feast.

"It's like a wildflower field of fish!" Kelly exclaimed breathlessly, more from the hard body that pressed against her than the wonder of the beauty below them.

"Have you ever been snorkeling?"

"No, I . . ." Kelly broke off as she saw the dark-skinned captain of the vessel grinning broadly at them. Pretending to follow a specific fish, she eased out of the warm enclosure Mac had set for her. "Oh, look at that one!" She pointed to a deep-blue fish with a train of red trailing from its gills. "She looks dressed for a ball." A darting glance revealed an amused contemplation on Mac's face that did not ease the wary feeling beginning to creep into the far recesses of her mind.

He gave her reprieve by walking over to the

captain. Kelly turned back to the water, staring blankly. Her heart was pounding in her chest. This was not going to be a vacation. It was going to be an exercise in torture. His well-intended show of the fish had managed to stir those damnable emotions that had rendered her shameless once before; and he had no idea! Thank goodness, she added with a discreet glance sideways.

The wind tossed his ink-blank hair around his bronzed face as if it enjoyed running its playful fingers through the thick, straight locks. The blue shirt, now dry and free of his narrow, belted waist, billowed away from his tapered upper torso. Like that, casual and relaxed instead of neat and business-like in a three-piece suit, he was irresistable, Kelly admitted reluctantly. Grey eyes crinkled in laughter at something the captain had said in rapid Spanish and suddenly they found hers. With a jerky smile at having been caught, she found a seat and began to read through the literature she had picked up at the information rack.

Chichen Itza, holy city of the Mayans. Kelly opened the brochure and became involved in the story of the Mayan people. During drought, they sought to appease the gods by throwing sacrifices into the great cenote, or underground lake, at the edge of the city. The most beautiful virgin (women's lib was never heard of, Kelly injected to herself with a wry grin) was fed the most exquisite foods, which were chased down by a tea made from the manta de la virgen, or white sapote leaf, containing a hallucinogenic drug called eleliuqui. At dawn, drugged, she was painted blue and dressed in an embroidered white ceremonial gown, her hair adorned with flowers; and led to the edge of the cenote by priests. Amid burning incense and incantations, the batabs threw her into the cenote, 180-feet across with 80-foot steep sides covered with slime and moss that led down to the constant 30-foot depths of murky water. Kelly shivered involuntarily as she pictured the scene in her mind.

"Are you cold?" Mac asked, an incredulous expression on his face as he offered her his arm.

The engine was shut down as the boat eased up to an immaculate white dock that jutted out into the water. Kelly shook her head.

"Women don't fare well in these parts, do they?" she joked, showing him the brochure.

"Ah, Chichen Itza," he chuckled, revealing his knowledge of the area. "I think you'll be alright as long as you watch what you drink."

Kelly laughed. "I'll keep that in mind."

Beyond the dock, at the top of a limestone-layered incline, was a sprawling white villa. Black-railed balconies made of iron lacework bespoke the Spanish influence as much as the gracefully slanted tiled roof. Casement windows had window boxes under them spilling trailing vines colored with exotic blossoms that draped over the stuccoed walls. There was no other sign of habitation on either side of it and Kelly guessed their client to be extremely wealthy to afford such a tropical paradise all for himself.

She permitted Mac to help her up to the dock. When she turned to take the cases, he shook his head and pointed beyond her to the two white-uniformed boys running out to meet them. There was a rapid exchange of Spanish before the boys bowed to her.

"Buenos tardes, Senora Mackenzie. Greetings to our villa."

"Welcome, Esteban," Mac corrected the younger of the two.

"Si, Don Jaime," the boy beamed, taking up Kelly's bags and trudging after his older brother before she could reply.

She gave Mac an impish grin. "They think we're married, Don Jaime," she mimicked.

Mac's arm slipped around her waist, his eyes studying her. "I'll straighten things out."

Kelly stepped away, maintaining her fecitious manner in spite of the serious race of blood coursing through her veins at his familiar move. "Well, you're not helping, sir," she added intentionally, before turning to follow the boys. "Why'd they call you that, anyway?" she asked suddenly, a frown knitting her smooth brow.

"I've been here quite a bit in the past," he confessed, guiding her up the dock after the boys.

"You know the owner then," she assumed, keeping a safe distance between them as she walked by his side, her own long legs having little difficulty keeping up with his.

"Yes, quite well."

Kelly would have questioned him further to satisfy her curiosity, but a stout woman came rushing up to them on the steps of the veranda with rails and posts that were adorned with the brightly-colored bougainvillea.

"Don Jaime! You make it too long to come back!" she said with a reproachful shake of her finger before hugging Mac about his waist, for that was nearly the full extent of her reach. Her head struck him about mid-chest.

"I've been busy, Teresa," he apologized, returning her gesture.

"That I can see." There was a twinkle in the dark eyes sweeping over her that made Kelly blush.

"Kelly, this is Teresa. She runs the villa. Teresa, this is Kelly, Custom Aero's best pilot."

"Why you not cook and have babies. Leave the man's work to the man," the woman demanded with a flick of her hand against Mac's chest.

Kelly looked down at the woman in astonishment. "Well, I . . . I like to fly." She glanced at Mac for help to see him grinning infuriatingly. "But someday I will . . . do what you said," she added, earning a reprieve from the indignant dark eyes of the servant.

"You'll love Teresa's cooking. There's no finer cook on the peninsula."

"In all of Mexico, you foolish boy!" The woman flashed with the twinkle that had never left her eyes in spite of her indignant tone. "Come, you must be tired from all that flying around. I take you upstairs," she said to Kelly, still disapproving of her occupation.

Before she left Kelly to change into her swimsuit, however, Teresa had put the girl at ease. The cook wanted to know what her favorite foods were, informing her that lobster was on the menu for the evening. Instead of permitting Kelly to unpack, Teresa made her sit on a chinz upholstered fainting couch that matched the soft tangerine of the king-size bed and drapes while she took her clothes out of the case and put them away in the rich mahogany chest of drawers or the closet, commenting favorably on her taste in wearing apparel. Kelly felt like a pampered belle of the South.

At least the housekeeper approved of something about her, Kelly mused wryly, adjusting the top to the halter of the bikini she had purchased for the trip. It was a delicate, dotted swiss, black on yellow, with small black bows at the side and the center of her top. It fit her slender form perfectly, but the areas of white that had not seen the tropical sun's rays made her feel somewhat self-conscious.

Oh well, she'd be tan by the week's end so that she'd be presentable on a public beach when she returned home. At least there was no one to see her here. If Mac was true to form, he'd be locked up with his client from now until departure.

She discovered that the balcony off her room ran the full length of the second floor and had steps that led down to an exquisitely furnished patio below that boasted a pool surrounded by lush greenery. Assuming a haughty pose, she imagined herself as the doña of the hacienda as she walked down the steps and past the pool, opting for the isolated beach nestled between upshoots of grey limestone that she had seen earlier from the boat as it rounded the finger of land the villa occupied.

Her graceful demeanor faltered as she picked her way down steps that had been carved into the rocky incline, a terry bath sheet rolled under her arm. A black rail anchored in the rock served to steady her. This was the life, she thought, as her toes sunk in the warm white sand of the beach. She kicked a spray of it in front of her as she walked to the water's edge. How often she'd been tempted to do the same at home, but the sun-bathers would have crucified her for such an atrocity.

Never having had a beach all to herself, Kelly gave into all the precocious temptations she'd previously denied. You are perverse, she admitted with a naughty grin as she dropped her swimsuit on the towel she'd spread out near the water's edge and ran into the gentle azure tide. Maybe she'd have no tan lines at all.

The water was refreshing as she swam under the

surface, her eyes taking in the glorious spectacle provided by nature. Some of its inhabitants fled like flittering slivers of silver light, while others stayed, swimming resentfully at a safe distance. After a rise for air, she went under again, her body singing in its freedom, as she moved gracefully through the water as if in her element.

She definitely wanted to try snorkeling, she decided as she came up again. Her feet found the bottom and she stood, the water streaming down to her hips at the water line as she tilted her head and tapped it lightly with her hand to clear out her ears.

"I really like your swimsuit."

Mac Mackenzie's voice drew her startled attention to the shore where he squatted by her towel, examining the small slips of yellow and black. With a mortified cry, Kelly dropped to her knees, her arms crossing her chest defensively. He straightened, a grin on his face as he stripped off his shirt and tossed it beside her swimsuit.

"Although I like you better as you are," he added wickedly, wading into the water toward her.

Kelly's eyes widened in panic. "Don't you have a business meeting?"

"Yes." He kept on toward her, enjoying her awkward predicament immensely.

She maneuvered so that her back was to him, remaining on her knees. She didn't see him, but she knew he was there. Her voice was shaking as she spoke, staring straight ahead at the mirror-blue sea beyond.

"This isn't business, Mac." She flinched as she felt his hands, warm against her shoulder.

"Yes, it is," he whispered, pressing against her, his hands keeping her from moving away. "You're fired."

"What!" Forgetting modesty, Kelly climbed to her feet and swung around to face him incredulously. "You can't do that!" Upon seeing his eyes staring at her breasts, firm and white against her tan, she crossed her arms again, flushing crimson. "Don't look at me like that!"

His hands locked on her shoulders. "I can, and I will," he told her huskily, drawing her closer in spite of her futile attempt to pull away.

"Mac, don't . . ."

Her plea was muted by the hard lips that took her mouth feverishly. Kelly tried desperately to escape the circle of iron holding her arms captive between them as his tongue forced its way past her defenses to exact unconditional surrender. She ordered her body to resist, but instead it molded against his muscled flesh, betraying her. Flames of desire licked at her defiant thoughts until they were consumed, leaving her weak in his arms.

"Mac," she moaned with one last stab of protest.

"No more business, love, strictly pleasure."

And she accepted it, not resisting when he gathered her in his arms and took her to the towel on the beach. She couldn't think, not now. She watched, mesmerized, as he stripped off his bathing trunks. Adonis. Black hair and bronzed sinew against a sky of cloudless blue. As her gaze dropped, she looked away shyly, shocked from her trance by the evidence of his need for her. When she would have rolled away, he was there, drawing her back with one leg across her flat stomach, where a need of her own became fired at the contact.

"You won't leave me this time?" she asked, her eyes inviting pools of sapphire, yet confused.

He shook her with his deep-throated chuckle. "My sweet innocent." His lips brushed hers gently. "I had not expected such fiery vixen behind that cool Valkyrie image of yours. You took me by surprise. However . . ."

Kelly took a sharp intake of breath as his lips moved to the erect peak of a breast and encircled it.

"Forewarned, I will not beat you to the finish line again, I promise."

His meaning registered in wonder on her face before the riotous sensations that spread throughout her body at his deliberate seduction made coherent thought impossible. She became aware of nothing but his scalding touch. It was sweet torture that drove her insane with the need to have him against her, skin welded against skin. Her hips rose to meet him as he catered to her pleas and weighted her down against the sand. The coarse hair of his legs caressed the silken skin of her inner thighs, making them clasp him in delight.

It wasn't enough. Kelly writhed in sweet agony as his hands committed every inch of her to his memory. Her body was like a tightly wound coil begging to be sprung free of the sexual tension he masterfully built. She implored him for release with a moan of kisses strung across his damp chest and when he obliged her with a lethal searing thrust, she nearly fainted, not from the unexpected pain, but from the rapture that followed.

"What fools those mortals be that called you the Valkyrie, my love, for you were Aphrodite in disguise."

Kelly snickered huskily at the romantic comparison as she lay in the cradle of his arms, reveling in this newfound intimacy. "You guys talked about me?"

"Beautiful women generate that sort of speculation," he admitted wryly, propping himself up on an elbow to look down at her. Her head used his arm as a pillow, her golden hair a shining contrast to his sun-darkened skin, while her body lay outstretched before him in its naked glory. "And I," he began poetically, "am the fortunate mortal who made such discovery and took you for my bride . . . a treasure lost to such ignorant knaves."

Kelly looked up at him lazily. "Is that a proposal?"

"In a way. I got all that wedding chaos, as you called it, out of the way beforehand." An arm tightened about her waist possessively. "Now, we can concentrate on our honeymoon. Does six weeks in Mexico appeal to you?"

"What?" she exclaimed in confusion.

Mac smiled patiently. "You remember all that paper signing this afternoon. It was certainly easier than showers and receptions and pasted-on smiles, wasn't it, Mrs. Mackenzie."

"You're kidding me," she accused, drawing up on her knees to stare down at him in disbelief.

Her expression of disbelief turned to incredulity as she recalled the man at the desk calling her senora. She had thought he had made a mistake and let it go, just as she had when the captain and the dock boys had made the same error. And then there had been Teresa's suggestive comment about cooking and babies. Yet, it was the intensity in the grey eyes that observed her silently that confirmed Mac's words.

"Cooking and babies!" she exploded, snatching up the first bit of cover she could lay hands on.

"Kelly . . ."

Kelly jumped back, gaining her footing at the same time as avoiding his reach. "Don't you touch me!" she warned, pulling his shirt on to cover her nakedness. "You've touched me enough!"

"For God's sake, be reasonable," Mac exclaimed, aggravation creeping into his tone as she picked up her bikini bottoms and struggled into them.

And he had fired her, she recalled, her ire growing as her toe caught in the leg of the panty, throwing her off balance. "And you can't fire me," she shouted angrily, hopping on one foot until the other foot slipped through the leg opening, "because I quit!"

"Now, just hold on . . ."

"And you can just sign some more papers to get us unmarried!"

"Will you stop ranting and listen to me a minute?" he demanded, his own temper slipping as he started to get up.

In a panic, Kelly kicked at him unexpectedly, catching him squarely in the chest and sending him sprawling back on the sand with an astonished oath. Before he could recover, she grabbed his wet swim trunks and threw them into the water. Her action guaranteeing safety for a moment, she darted up the hill toward the towering villa, ignoring his command to come back. He could command until he was blue in the face as far as she was concerned. She was going to pack her things and go home.

EIGHT

"Open this door!"

Mac found the balcony door locked and now pounded loudly on the corridor entrance to her room. Kelly watched the hinges shake as she stuffed her clothes into her suitcase, trying her best to ignore him. While they had had their quiet interlude on the beach, the servants had brought in his clothes and put them with hers. All so neatly planned . . . and she had not suspected a thing!

"You can't go anywhere unless I say so, Kelly. I have the keys to the Jeep, and we are miles from any village with dangerous jungle in between. The boat won't be back until next week with supplies, and the waters are shark-infested beyond the reef."

My God, it sounds like a horror movie, she moaned inwardly. She looked through tear-glazed eyes at her suitcase, her clothing a wad of wrinkles jammed in simulated leather. She'd trusted him . . . really trusted him.

"I won't take you anywhere until we talk," the terse voice on the other side of the door threatened.

Her head jerked up. "Ken was right about you, you . . . you opportunist!" She furiously stomped over to the door and hit it. "He said you took what you wanted without regard for others and that I'd end up in . . . I hate you! I hate you! I hate you!" she finished, sobs making her speech incoherent.

It wasn't until they had subsided that she realized Mac was no longer at the door. Its smooth wood was cool to her tear-scalded face as she leaned against it in an unaccustomed helplessness. What on earth could she do? Idly, she picked at the shirt that covered her shoulders. Well, whatever she did, she needed to shower and dress first. Then, perhaps she could think more clearly.

A gentle tapping came on the door as she pulled her white, cotton knit tank dress over her head after her bath. There was a dull ache in her temples from her extreme distress and she held her fingers to them as she inquired who it was.

"It is Teresa, senora. I have brought up some tea. Perhaps it make you feel better."

Cautiously, Kelly cracked the door and then swung it wide to permit Teresa to enter with the tray, once she determined the servant was alone. The dark-skinned woman looked at Kelly's suitcase and her mouth thinned in quiet disapproval;

yet, it softened slightly when she saw her swollen, red eyes and drawn face.

"You drink this tea and take these aspirin. Then maybe you feel better."

It would take more than tea and aspirin, Kelly thought morosely, but she gave the woman a little smile of thanks. "It was kind of you to think of me, Teresa."

"Oh, not for me," the woman denied emphatically. "Don Jaime thinks you not feel well and sends me to you. He is a good man, Don Jaime."

Kelly looked at the woman suspiciously. Did she know what Mac had done, she wondered. "Teresa . . ."

"Si, senora?"

"If I were to become very ill, how would we get a doctor? I mean, if the nearest village is miles through the jungle, what would you do?"

"Not to worry, senora. We would call on the radio in Don Jaime's biblioteca . . . library . . . and a doctor would fly in by seaplane."

Kelly blanched. Don Jaime's library? "This is Mac's house?" she questioned incredulously.

"Who else's, senora?" the woman asked equally. "Your husband is a very wealthy man, as was his dear abuela . . . grandmama. This was her family home and hers before she died." The woman made a cross over her buxom chest.

That explained his dark complexion and fluency in Spanish. Mac Mackenzie was part-Mexican. It was odd that he had never mentioned it, but then there was a lot that he had never told her about himself . . . a lot she did not know about her own husband.

Kelly downed the pills gratefully with water from the bathroom as the woman poured the tea. She looked at the reddish-brown liquid and gave a slightly hysterical laugh as she recalled the story on the brochure, astounding the servant who looked at her oddly.

"Do you have any blue paint?"

"Senora?"

"Never mind," Kelly sighed, dismissing the ridiculous comparison. "I'd like to rest."

At her hint, Teresa nodded and started for the door. "Supper will be in one hour. I know you feel better after that." She hesitated in the entrance uneasily. "Senora, Don Jaime told me to tell you that if you do not come to dinner, he will bring it to you in here. He does have a key to his own room, senora."

Kelly stared miserably at the closed door after the cook left. Exquisite foods were in order, she supposed. Drugged or not, the tea relaxed her. She set the tray aside on the bed and reclined on the pillows. A trapped feeling seemed to choke her as she closed her eyes. No way to escape, a voice echoed against a chorus that asked why she wanted to.

Teresa awakened her at the dinner hour. Kelly had drifted off in restless slumber that left her more fatigued than she had been earlier. She got up and brushed her hair, not caring whether she looked attractive or not. A quick splash of cold water was all the attention she gave her face, ignoring the cosmetic case on the dresser. Trembling hands smoothed the soft cotton knit of her dress as she descended the stairs behind Teresa, a mutinous expression on her face.

She took careful note of her surroundings as she passed through the tiled foyer, glancing in each open door to identify the rooms. A half-smile touched her lips as she saw one lined with rows of books and furnished in burgundy leather. The biblioteca, she thought with satisfaction.

Her smile faded as she entered a candlelit room where Mac, now dressed in a flaxen suit and silk shirt, rose to meet her. His expression was inscrutable as he took her arm and seated her next to him at one end of a long banquet table. He poured a chilled wine from an unlabeled bottle, which Kelly suspected may have been bottled and aged locally. She accepted the fragile goblet, studying the dark red color through the crystal in the candlelight.

"It contains no sapote brew," Mac assured her, his voice edged with sarcasm.

"Pity . . . it might make this more tolerable."

"Ah, the Valkyrie returns."

Kelly sipped the wine, her eyes flashing over the ruby contents to his frosty grey ones. It was a semi-sweet concoction, soothing to her throat that had gone dry.

"And by her look, she craves my dead body so she might take me to the great hall of lost heroes."

Kelly was saved a retort by the entrance of Teresa and one of the small boys that had brought in the luggage earlier. Exquisite did not quite do justice to the food they spread before them. Lobster, steamed in banana leaves, fresh fruit salad, and wild rice with mushrooms tempted the appetite Kelly would have sworn she did not have. Teresa hovered over them, watching anxiously for approval so Kelly could not possibly have refused to eat everything on her plate for fear of hurting the cook's feelings.

The bulk of the conversation was between Mac and Teresa as the older woman caught him up on the local happenings. He had many friends on Quintana Roo, mostly owners of the sisal or hene-quin plantations, the product of which was made into hemp for rope and twine. Kelly listened to them sullenly. Mac insisted that Teresa keep speaking in English for her benefit when the woman would lapse into a frustrated Hispanic rattle. The meal came to an end with bocaditas del cielo, delicious caramel custards called "mouthfuls of heaven."

As the servants left with the dishes from the table, Mac pulled out her chair for her. "Shall we retire to the salon for an after-dinner drink?"

"I came down here as you ordered. Now I just want to go to bed . . . alone!" she added at the suggestive rise of his brow.

"You are in our room," he pointed out dryly.

"Then you sleep there and I'll sleep on the beach . . . or on the sofa . . ." she added, coloring at his slow-spreading smile, "or anywhere you are not!" she finished awkwardly.

"How long do these tantrums usually last? I haven't had much dealings with children."

Kelly clenched her jaw at his insult and spun on her heel, refusing to dignify his comment with a retort. As she found her way back to her room, she kept listening for Mac to follow, but he did not. Perhaps he was going to give her her wish after all, she thought, locking the bedroom door behind her as an exercise of caution. Then, recalling Teresa's information that he had a key, she unlocked it.

What a horrid mess, she groaned, dropping on to the fainting couch. She was married to a man she hardly knew. If only he had given her time to get used to the idea . . . and him. She was attracted to him, but marriage meant forever to her; and forever and Mac Mackenzie just didn't seem to go together. Besides, physical attraction and love were not always one and the same.

She would get back home and then, if he really wanted her, he could court her conventionally. Of course, she would have to get another job. There was no way she could maintain a professional relationship with him now . . . not after today. She leaned back against the cushion, her mind exhausted from the shock and confusion of the past hours. But first, she had to get away.

The hours dragged by as Kelly watched the beautiful rosewood clock that graced a shelf on the wall. Teresa had checked in and offered to help her dress for bed. Kelly declined her offer, taking out a nightgown and tossing it on the bed as if she were about to turn in so as not to alert any suspicion in the woman. When the servant had gone, she tucked the garment back in the luggage and zipped it.

The clock struck twelve midnight against a background of thunder. Kelly had observed the storm clouds thickening in the evening sky like heavy billows of black smoke blotting out the moon and stars that had twinkled earlier in the night. Shortly after two, she had just put her hand on the door knob when lightning struck, illuminating the room sharply and making her start.

Kelly waited to see if the thunderburst caused anyone to stir, but upon opening the door quietly, she detected only the stillness of a sleeping house. With light treads, she made her way down the steps and into the library where the radio was kept. Reception would be awful with the storm, but not impossible, and she was desperate.

She closed the door behind her and found her way by the erratic light of the storm to where the radio sat on a shelf near the window. She put on the headphones and began to turn the dials. There was static on static, occasionally interrupted by electronic voice transmissions that became garbled more frequently than not.

After half an hour, the storm began to recede. Kelly tried once more, selecting a frequency to summon the marine band operator. Keeping her voice as low as possible, she spoke clearly and succinctly into the mike, directing her call to Dan Mooney. It was another half an hour before the call got through. At the sound of Uncle Dan's voice crackling through the earphones accepting the charges, Kelly cried.

"Uncle Dan, this is Kelly. I'm married to Mac Mackenzie," she blurted out brokenly.

Static indicated his interruption. "Congratulations, nothing . . . make . . . happier at three o'clock in the morning."

"No, you don't understand," she said, her voice trembling with frustration at the distorting static.

"Is something . . . damned radio . . . something wrong?"

Kelly shrieked as the headset was snatched from her in the darkness. Mac Mackenzie put the mike to his lips and activated it, riveting her to the chair with a frosty warning.

"Hello . . . hello, Dan?"

"Congratulations, son! You take care . . . girl, now."

"I will, sir. She just couldn't wait to tell you. Sorry we woke you." Mac's voice was cheerful, but his look was venomous as he glared at Kelly.

"Worth . . . up for. Sure you . . . better things to do . . . talk to old man. Love . . . both."

"Goodbye, sir."

"Bye."

Kelly paled as the radio went dead. Mac turned off all the dials and set the headphones gently down with a strain that showed during a silent flash of lightning in the distance in the tense muscles jerking in his jaw.

"This has gone far enough."

His words rumbled like the far-off thunder as his fingers latched about her arms and drew her to her feet, biting painfully into her flesh. As Kelly began to struggle, he shook her roughly, snapping her head back and forth until she was nearly senseless.

"What did you hope to do by upsetting that man at this hour of the night? My God, what did you think I would do to you? What kind of man do you think I am, Kelly?"

"You tricked me!" she gasped, groping for her balance and latching onto the lapels of his robe.

"I prefer to think of it more as a surprise. You would have accepted my proposal on the beach this afternoon and you know it, so what's the difference?"

"You never asked me," she said in a timid voice, ceasing her resistance in defeat. "I never had a choice."

His hands moved to her hips, pulling her against

him as his eyes burned into hers. "You could have said no this afternoon . . ."

"No, I couldn't!" she denied hotly. Her eyes widened and she inhaled a sharp breath at her inadvertent admission.

Mac suddenly crushed her in his arms, his body shaking with amusement. "Don't ever play poker, or engage in espionage, my blatantly-honest love." He kissed the top of her head. "Your boyfriend was right in one respect. When I see something I want, I do take it . . . but not against its will. I wanted you the minute you told me to shut up and kiss you when strangulation seemed more the order of the day . . . but Hudson was in the way. I suspected you didn't love him and you confirmed my suspicion when you asked me to love you the night you tossed him out on his ear."

Kelly could not believe her ears. Her mind floundered in confusion. "But why didn't you ask me . . . why did you trick me?"

"You don't think I was going to give Hudson a chance to get back in good with you, did you? Call it opportunism if you will, but I took the chance and I think I've won," he added, lifting her face to his. "Don't tell me you don't want this any less than me."

Lips that were tender brushed hers at first, tasting, teasing until she responded. She did want him. Her initial reaction had been one of shock, not really reflective of what she actually felt. She would have married him. Yes had been on the tip of her tongue, waiting for the properly-phrased question. The very initiative he demonstrated in marrying her was one of the things she admired in him. The fact that he married her before taking her made him more a gentleman.

"At the end of six weeks, my love, if you still want a divorce, I give you my word of honor, you shall have it."

Once again she'd been the fool, but tonight, she would make it up to him, Kelly vowed, shyly tasting his mouth with her own tongue. Encouraged by the tightening of his arms about her, she plowed her fingers through the crop of hair on his chest, seeking out the masculine peaks that drew up under her playful touch. Recalling his sweet torment of her breasts, she moved her mouth to them, circling with her tongue as he had done and nipping mischievously until his breathing was ragged. The discovery that this torment could work both ways inspired her, but before she could proceed any further, she found herself scooped off the floor.

"Tonight is our wedding night, Ace. Shall we fly to our room?"

Kelly nuzzled his chest and laughed softly. "You're crazy, Mac Mackenzie."

"Over you, Mrs. Mackenzie."

Her heart sang as he carried her up the steps and instinctively she knew it would not take six weeks to know if she loved this man.

How quickly the days passed! Snorkeling became

an adventuresome pastime, usually ending up with a romantic picnic for two on one of the many isolated beaches. On one occasion, Mac had just built a palmetto fire with a platform of twigs over it, when a boatload of young people bound for a beach party came up on them. Before the afternoon was over, three other similar boats had beached for a riotous time. Lobster and fish were broiled and smoked over the open fire while gin and tonics were the drink of the day. Argentine paté and Danish sausages, Stilton cheese from Belize, all became an international spread as the parties combined. When their captain set sail for Villa Bianca, Kelly swayed in Mac's arms, somewhat tipsy from the afternoon of liquor, sun, sea, and festive camaraderie, and watched the dolphins dancing on the blue-flame dance floor against the background of the Caribbean sunset.

Spearfishing off Celerain and a subsequent alligator hunt became their most daring excursion. Surrounded by a forest of multi-toned green, sprayed well with insect repellent and ill at ease at being the only woman in the party, Kelly kept close to her husband in the row boat that slipped silently through the moonlit water cutting the darkness with a floodlight. Night sounds, herons soaring into flight, a creaking bough under a sleepy pelican as he shifted his heavy weight, the cries of a wild duck, all sent shivers of apprehension up her spine and tightened her grasp on the taut bicep beside her.

And so she remained until Mac stood up and speared what appeared to be an innocent log with a forceful thrust. Pressed against the opposite side of the craft, only inches away in reality, Kelly watched with wide eyes, fearful and fascinated, as the reptile spun in the water, thrashing and splashing water on the occupants of the boat. Having brought his own gear, Mac drew a pistol and finished off the agonized animal, but the real horror came when Kelly realized for the first time that it was to be carried back to the encampment in their boat. It was the longest boat ride that she could ever remember, her nerves strung to their limit with the cold brown-green corpse on the deck between her feet.

Whether dining intimately in an open-air nightclub built over an underground lake or rowing through the wild lagoons of the peninsula, Kelly had never known such happiness. Memories of each moment were tucked away as a treasure in her mind. Each day she found herself more in love with Mac, wondering how she could ever have doubted him. He had given love a new meaning that could never apply to any other man, and had taught her secrets about herself that she had never dreamed existed.

"So, how does it feel?"

Kelly lifted her eyelids lazily, shaken from her reverie by her husband's voice against her ear. "What's that?" she asked, lifting her head from his shoulder where it had rested comfortably during the takeoff of the plane Mac had chartered to San Miguel. The island trip was his penance for the alligator hunt.

"Riding as a passenger for a change," Mac teased, drawing her head back and kissing her on the forehead playfully. "I like that dress. It has all sorts of possibilities."

Kelly glanced down at the tank dress she had worn on more than one occasion since their wedding night. She had thought it odd that he asked her to wear it, but it had not bothered her. It was cool and serviceable for travel. "Thank you, sir. I try to buy things that can either be dressed up or down with accessories. It helps stretch the budget a little."

"That's not what I meant," he told her deviously, one hand slipping boldly under the straps and shoving them off her tanned shoulders with little effort.

"Mac, will you behave yourself!" she chastised with a giggle, her eyes darting nervously to the curtained entrance area that separated the sealed cockpit from the passenger section, which was empty except for the two of them.

As she began to put them back, he stopped her. "I think we should start our own Mile High Club right here," he suggested, a wicked gleam in his eyes as they delighted in her startled reaction.

Kelly recovered quickly. Trying to maintain a stern demeanor, she scolded, "You said you did not think that sort of thing was a good idea, as I recall . . . and besides, the pilot . . .''

"I said that I thought the pilot should keep his mind on his flying," he corrected, unfastening her seatbelt. "And since neither of us is piloting this aircraft," he began, pulling her into his lap, "and the pilot is safely enclosed in his own little world of instruments, his mind strictly on flying . . .''

"Mac!''

Kelly tried to catch the hands that tugged at her dress, her heart beating rapidly in knowledge that she could not win . . . nor did she want to. Her struggle was convincingly valiant, regardless of the snickers that periodically slipped through her facade of indignant protest. She loved him. She loved his spontaneity, his touch, his passion that fed her own. Feeling decidedly wicked, she surrendered to the flames of desire that engulfed them both.

When she stepped off the plane, she could neither help her sheepish expression nor her crimson blush when the pilot asked if they had enjoyed their flight and was grateful to see the hotel bus making its way toward them. Mac said little on the way to the beachfront complex. He didn't have to. All he had to do was look at her to break the cool front of the fascinated tourist she had assumed.

There was a message to call Custom Aero when they checked in at the desk. Once in their room, Kelly hurried to shower and changed for a dinner party a friend of Mac's was throwing in their honor at a backyard salon, while Mac called in at the plant. He usually checked in every other day or so to keep tap on what was going on. A week after he had announced their marriage to Midge, a gigantic arrangement of flowers arrived on the boat, sent from the gang at Custom Aero in congratulations. A card signed by almost every employee in the plant accompanied it, so many signatures that Kelly could hardly make out the bride and groom on the front or the verse.

When she came out of the bathroom, her hair wrapped turban-fashion in a towel and another towel encircling her body, Mac sat grimly on the edge of the bed, the receiver still in his hand. A sixth sense of terrible dread came over her as she sat alongside him, asking with her eyes what she feared to voice.

"We have to go back right away, Kelly," he began, replacing the receiver in its cradle.

"Has there been an accident?" she found the nerve to ask. Extreme safety measures were always used in testing the modified aircraft, but sometimes the most unexpected things happened.

Mac shook his head as he looked at her, his eyes full of sympathy. "Dan Mooney died this morning of a heart attack."

Kelly jerked as if the blow had been physical. Uncle Dan dead? She shook her head, refusing to accept what her husband was telling her. Hadn't they just spoken to him a few days before? She recalled how he had laughed boisterously at her comic rendition of the alligator hunt. He'd sounded great, talking with enthusiasm about a small reception he wanted to have for them at the Hangar. A blade, sharp and lethal, lodged in her throat.

"Ma . . . ac," she accused painfully, her eyes blurring so that his image was hazy as he gathered her in his arms.

"I know, love. I know," he whispered as the dam of tears gave way, holding her tightly to absorb the convulsive sobs of her grief.

They did not go to the dinner party that night. Mac called and explained the circumstances to his friend who assured them he understood completely and offered his condolences. After a meal of club sandwiches and soup in their room, which Kelly hardly touched, Mac took her to bed, holding her tenderly in his arms as she cried herself to sleep over the loss of the man who had been like a father to her.

NINE

It had been a nightmare—the flag flying at half-staff as they flew into the Custom Aero airfield, the funeral, the aftermath of well-wishers who offered congratulations and condolences in the same breath. Mac had flown the Citation back, Kelly accompanying him in the copilot's seat. She didn't want to be left alone in the back of the plane. He had also taken charge of the arrangements for Uncle Dan's only surviving relative, a sister from Tulsa. Appropriately, the plant was shutdown so that employees could attend the services for the founder, and a large dinner was given afterward in the plant by the women's auxiliaries of the many clubs he belonged to.

Kelly found her husband a pillar of strength and managed to come through stiffly. Now, seated in Custom Aero's private attorney's office with Uncle Dan's sister, Rose, a slender well-dressed woman with silvered hair curled close to a gracefully aged face, she listened numbly as his attorney read the last will and testament. She never dreamed Uncle Dan would leave her anything, although he often offered to help her financially. She had never accepted any money that she had not reimbursed in full, so when the lawyer summoned her to the reading of the will, she had been upset all over again.

"To Kelly Benson, the remaining shares of Custom Aero, coming to forty-nine percent of the corporate stock."

Kelly's mouth opened in astonishment as the words sunk in.

"Kelly, I have a personal message for you from Mr. Mooney," the attorney was telling her. "Do you have any objection if the others present listen?"

Her eyes stung as she shook her head. She could not imagine anything that either Mac or Rose should not be privy to. Mac's reassuring squeeze of her hand, helped steady her shaky emotions.

The attorney nodded and proceeded to read. "My dear, independent Kelly," he began. "I regret that I never had the courage to tell you what I have to say. I promised your mother that I would not, but she, too, is gone and I can see no reason that you should not know. You are the daughter my own Vanessa could not bear me. Your mother carried you when she married my best friend and closest associate, George Benson. It was a weak moment of passion you have never given me cause to regret. No, your father did not know. Coward that I was, I could not face him with the truth, either. Please forgive me and know that you always have had and will have my love." The lawyer cleared his throat. "Of course, it is signed by Mister . . . er . . . your father."

"Oh, my dear," Rose Mooney Sturgis exclaimed, turning to the girl next to her and giving her a lilac-scented hug. "I always wondered, the way my Danny talked about you."

Kelly could not speak. Uncle Dan, her father? Oh God, it explained so much—the cool distance he always kept between himself and Marta Benson, the constant concern over Kelly's financial situation, her job and privileges at the plant. There were trips he and his wife had taken her on as a child and gifts they had given her as her godparents. She couldn't imagine loving him more if she had known.

Kelly went through the motions of thanking the lawyer, grateful for the strong arm that guided her out of the office and down the hall to the office that now labeled James Mackenzie as president. Mac engaged in light conversation with Rose as he gathered up the luggage she had left in his office. She had checked out of her hotel and was to take a private flight back to Tulsa after the reading of the will.

"Kelly dear, you and this handsome husband of yours must come to Tulsa to visit me. I feel as though I have been cheated of a lovely niece for the past twenty-odd years and we have a lot of time to make up for.''

Kelly was embraced again. She backed away as the slender woman released her. ''Thank you, we will, Mrs. Sturgis.''

''Aunt Rose, dear . . . and you can call me that, too, young man,'' she teased, light twinkling in crinkled eyes.

''I'd be honored,'' Mac grinned, glancing with concern at the pallor beneath Kelly's tropical tan. ''Kelly, why don't you stay here in my office while I see Rose to her plane?''

''That would be nice, if you don't mind, Aunt Rose. I . . . I feel a little shaky to tell the truth,'' Kelly admitted with a strained smile.

''Of course, not!'' the woman declared as if the idea were absurd. ''You've had a terrible shock, dear. I'll just give you my good-bye kiss right here.'' She planted a red lip print on Kelly's cheek and waved for Mac to follow her as she briskly walked through the door.

''I'll be right back,'' he promised as he turned sideways to maneuver the cases through the entrance.

Drained, Kelly curled up in the large leather armchair that sat behind the executive desk, the skirt of the navy dress neatly tucked in around her slender legs. Her mind drifted to the words Uncle Dan had said at the wedding. He was on her side. Always, he had said, and to remember that when he was gone. Her throat constricted, but her swollen eyes could shed no more tears. They burned to, but she had cried them dry.

"The master ordered a drink for his lady," a masculine voice broke into her thoughts, making her start.

Kelly looked up at Ken Hudson warily. Dear God, she couldn't stand a confrontation now. Yet, he seemed pleasant enough as he opened the canned soda and placed it on the desk in front of her along with a set of blueprints intended for Mac.

"I was on my way to deliver this report when I ran into Midge. I told her I'd bring in your drink," he explained at the questioning look she gave him. "I wanted to tell you how sorry I am, Kelly . . . about many things, but right now, about Dan. I know how close you were to him."

"Thank you, Ken," she managed, before taking a drink of the soda to soothe her aching throat. "I know you liked him, too."

Ken sat on the edge of the desk facing her, his eyes wandering to her hands that worked nervously in her lap. "No ring?"

"What? Oh!" she said, following his meaning. "We haven't had time to get one, I guess."

Her tanned face began to develop a definite rose tint as she realized how her answer sounded. Before she could say anything else, Ken leaned over and gave her an affectionate buss on the cheek, freezing her motionless in shock.

"You haven't changed a bit . . . just as innocently tactless as ever," he laughed, rising to his feet.

"A beguiling trait I'm particularly fond of," Mac Mackenzie's voice interrupted from the open doorway. A lopsided grin met Ken's astonished look as Mac leaned against the jamb, eyes keenly observing him with inscrutable depth. "Is that the set of prints you've been working on?"

Ken nodded soberly, uncertain as to what his employer was thinking.

Kelly watched with the same uncertainty. It was as if two bulls were sizing each other up for a charge. A charge that was not to take place because Mac crossed the room and picked up the packet Ken had dropped in his basket.

"I doubt there'll be any changes, but I'll go through the exercise of looking them over." He looked up at Ken evenly. "You do good work, Ken. I liked that concept you used in St. Louis . . . damned innovative."

"Thank you, sir," Ken stammered, as caught off guard by Mac's compliment as by his unexpected appearance. "Uh, and congratulations," he added, offering his hand which Mac accepted firmly.

"Thanks. Now, if you don't mind, I'd like to take my wife out of here. She's been under enough strain without having to stay in this madhouse much longer."

Kelly went willingly to Mac's side as Ken made a prompt exit. She welcomed her husband's arm as he escorted her out of the building to his silver-blue Mercedes. As the engine sprang to life, she looked at him in a mixture of wonder and admiration.

"You are really special," she told him, leaning across the seat and hugging him. "Thanks."

"If I have to box every male that looks at you longingly, I'll be too busy to enjoy what they're envious of . . . and Hudson's good enough to try to save. Now," he said, resting his right arm on the back of the seat and facing her. "Do you want to go back to our apartments or ride around for a while and unwind?"

Kelly laughed as his expression changed from bored to bright with each suggestion. She didn't blame him for not wanting to go back home. It had been chaos, living in two apartments, neither of which was big enough to hold both their things combined. Every time one of them needed something, it was in the other place. Mac had teased her about being a traffic hazard, running back and forth between them in her bathrobe for an article of clothing she had forgotten.

"Unwind," she said, sinking down in the bucketseat of dark-blue leather.

"Well, let's pop the top and go."

He lowered the convertible roof and doffed the dark jacket to his suit and his tie. With them bundled behind his seat, he loosened his collar and merged out on the highway. Kelly studied him from the protection of her sunglasses. His hair was brushed off his face by the air rushing over the windshield, revealing a classic profile, hard and clean cut. White, even teeth contrasted with his dark complexion as he smiled lazily, maneuvering in and out of the traffic.

They passed through several developments, Kelly admiring the homes situated on plushly landscaped lots. Some were more distinctive than others. The further they drove, the larger the lots were and the grander the houses. They turned into a new subdivision that was wooded for the most part, with only a few completed homes near the entrance. As they moved deeper into the woods, she saw some construction work and then more finished houses beyond.

"Pretty area, isn't it?" Mac commented as he slowed the car to remain on the outside of a circle they had entered. "That's a nice one there," he added, pointing to a two-story home with a French motif.

"Beautiful. I love the little blue balconies under the front windows. It looks like Cinderella's castle."

It did. It was made of white brick that sparkled in the sunlight as if sprinkled with the dust of a fairy godmother's wand, and topped with a dark blue-black mansard roof. There was a double front door, painted the same powder blue as the copper-flashed balconies that hung on either side of the two-storied columned portico. A larger balcony graced the double French doors above the main

entrance. The freshly planted shrubs needed imagination to reach storybook proportion, but Kelly
could picture what it would look like with a few
good years of proper care. The new lawn looked
like soft emerald velvet, the tiny blades of grass
fragile and vibrant in the afternoon breeze.

"Want to look inside?"

Kelly looked at Mac in surprise. "How . . . I
mean, we might get arrested, peeking in through
the windows."

"Midge'll bail us out. Come on."

He led her up a winding stone walk that led
from the circle to the door and rang the doorbell.

"What are you doing?" Kelly exclaimed, glancing over her shoulder uneasily.

"Senora! Don Jaime! We have been waiting by
the window!"

"Teresa?" Kelly was suddenly crushed against
the full bosom of the housekeeper whose short,
wiry arms rendered her breathless with the over-
zealous greeting.

"Pobrecita, we have so much for you," Teresa
cooed, stroking Kelly's hair sympathetically. "But
you like your new house. Oh!" Teresa put her
hand over her mouth, wide eyes darting to Mac
in apology.

"New house! Mac?" Kelly echoed, turning to
her husband.

"Midge found it while we were in Tulum, and
Teresa has been setting up house for the past

week," he explained, his face apprehensive as he watched for her reaction.

"But how did you know I like this type of architecture?"

"Susie helped Midge by showing her a house you had flipped over in a magazine. Care to look around?"

"Is there anything you haven't thought of?" she asked, throwing herself into his arms and clinging tightly to him. He was more wonderful than she could imagine. "I love you so much, Mac Mackenzie!"

"Madame, this public display of affection is going to start the neighbors talking," he whispered, nibbling at her ear. "And I believe this is the procedure."

Kelly wrapped her arms about his neck as he picked her up and carried her over the threshold. She looked around in awe at the grand staircase circling down from the second floor around the perimeter of the round foyer.

"Oh, Mac!" she marveled.

Warm oak planking, shining with a new finish that still scented the air, covered the floor and the corridor that ran under the wrought iron railed staircase. As Kelly walked through slowly, followed by her husband and a just-as-anxious Teresa, she examined each of the large rooms. A neutral caramel carpet had been installed throughout the first floor where the natural wood floors left off, and all the walls and ceilings were painted white.

Thin white voile curtains covered the reproduction leaded glass casements.

"I left the decorating to you. You can choose whatever colors and furniture you please. Here is a checkbook and your own set of charge cards."

"Mac!" Kelly exclaimed incredulously. She raised her hands to her face, unable to comprehend what was happening. It was too much.

"This project should keep you busy a few weeks. I know I'll have to keep thinking of ways to prevent you from missing your job," he added with a mischievous wink.

"And my kitchen, it is wonderful!" Teresa injected, taking her arm and dragging Kelly through a set of cafe doors into a cook's paradise.

Oak cabinets ran from floor to ceiling over and under the soft, blue slate counter top. Again, with the exception of a neutral tile above the counter, the walls were white. A two-leveled work island in the center with a copper framed hood, where Teresa had hung a myriad of pots and pans, hosted a stainless steel stove and grill on the upper level and an eating bar on the lower one. Oak stools with cushions that matched the counter provided seating.

"It is wonderful, Teresa," Kelly conceded, stepping closer to Mac and slipping her arm around his waist to lean against him. "But not as wonderful as Don Jaime."

"And now to my favorite part of the house," Mac remarked suggestively, suddenly hoisting her up on his shoulder. "What time is dinner, Teresa?"

"Madre de Dios, you want dinner when we got no table?" the cook exclaimed, her laughter mingling with that of the frolicking couple.

"My wife needs to keep her strength up!" Mac called over his shoulder as he carried Kelly through the swinging doors.

"Then I call for the pizza man and he bring it!" Teresa answered defiantly. "And you eat out of the box! Aye!"

Kelly laughed so hard her sides were aching by the time Mac put her down at the top of the winding steps in front of the French doors that led to the larger balcony. Poor Teresa would have an apoplectic fit if her prankish husband were to continue. Kelly could imagine what the poor woman had already been through, having been moved to a foreign country to set up house, starting from scratch.

"The guest rooms are all down that way on both sides of the corridor. They are all the same, white and empty," Mac stated in a tour-guide tone. "However, to our right is the master suite. It is white also, but it does have some furniture."

He swung open a door to a room that ran the full depth of the house. A fireplace was in the center, directly over the one in the living room below. Beautiful moldings and panels made up the hearth wall. At one end, a large mattress and box spring lay on the floor, made up with bed linens and pillows.

"At least it has the bare necessities."

"You're incorrigible!" Kelly accused as he led her over to the makeshift bed.

"Get your mind out of the gutter, wife. I have absolutely unselfish motives."

He pushed her back on the bed and fell down beside her, rolling over on his elbow. "Now, I want you to take a nap . . . alone," he added wryly, "or you won't get any sleep." He gave her a brief kiss and got up suddenly.

Kelly sobered. "Where are you going?"

"Teresa and I are going to our apartments to gather up our clothes and whatever we need to stay over. Tomorrow our furniture will be moved."

"You're leaving me alone?" she asked, feeling foolish about her sudden qualms at staying in the big house by herself. It was like a modern castle.

"We'll lock you up safe and sound, I promise. Goodnight, Cinderella."

Mac pulled the comforter up over her and with another kiss, he was gone. Kelly stared after him and sighed contentedly. Cinderella. That's just what she felt like. A few weeks ago she was struggling to make ends meet and now she was Mrs. Mac Mackenzie and an heiress. Oh, Uncle Dan, if only you could have lived to see how happy I am. Her throat tightened at the memory of the rotund, energetic figure who was her real father.

If only you could see, the thought echoed as she closed her eyes and gave into the fatigue of her mourning.

After a hectic weekend of arranging furniture and putting away their things, Kelly contacted a decorator Midge recommended. While Mac worked, Kelly began a grueling routine of choosing the decor and appropriate furniture for each room, trying to work around those pieces they already had. It might have been easier to give the woman carte blanche to do as she wished with Kelly's general taste in mind, but Kelly insisted on picking everything out herself, taking the designer's advice into consideration. She was so used to working on a budget that old habits were not easily shed. Within weeks the house was developing into a lovely home with warm and fresh colors that welcomed visitors, which they had plenty of.

She finished the master bedroom, living room, and dining room first. At Mac's insistence, she used their older bedroom suites in the guest rooms and furnished their private room with hand-painted reproduction furniture of French design. Shirred silk in beige with delicate blue flowers set the theme for the drapes, spread, and plump upholstered loveseat and window seats. A two-level dressing table with an Italian marble top was her favorite piece, over which hung a gilded French mirror topped with Chinese jade flowers. Coordinating wall paper pulled the decor together for an elegantly romantic effect.

They had slept in nearly every room upstairs in order to keep out of the way of the painters and paperhangers that filled the house with the odors of fresh paint and paste until Kelly could not stomach a full meal there unless all the windows and doors were open to air it out. She ran herself ragged trying to keep up with the energetic decorator who had endless sources for the just the right paper or piece to do this room or that. Yet, she managed to revive when her husband came home or when he managed to catch her between errands to meet him for lunch.

Susie, who was busy decorating her own home on a stringent budget, accompanied her on many of her treasure hunts to antique shops where Kelly found interesting knickknacks to complete the grand, but homey, effect she tried to attain. They giggled and carried on like schoolgirls in spite of the shocked owners who watched them warily, lest they be tempted to help themselves to a valuable piece of glass. However, when Kelly found something and presented the card bearing Mac's name, the haughty attitude changed swiftly to one of patronization.

"God, did you see the look on her face when you said charge it to my husband?" Susie laughed, mimicking the woman with the dyed-red hair and heavily madeup face.

"Well, we hardly look as if we could afford the brass fittings on the darned thing, let alone the whole piece," Kelly reminded her friend, glancing down at her blue jeans and fashionably wrinkled shirt. Knowing that they would be going through some of the less-distinguished shops, which smelled of must and mildew and brandished dust and dirt in the "buy-as-is" sections, they had worn casual clothing. "But I think it will be beautiful next to the front entrance," she added, picturing the oak hall tree against the muted green-on-ivory print of the paper she had had put up earlier.

"How about lunch?" Susie suggested, pointing to a fast-food place across the street.

"Sounds good. Maybe I can eat without tasting paint," Kelly remarked sarcastically. "But at least all that's done now."

They left Kelly's Thunderbird parked in front of the antique shop and walked to the restaurant. After helping themselves to the salad bar, they found a seat near the window under a curved sun roof of tinted glass. Kelly picked at the salad, her mind searching for a place for the small wall cupboard with the punched tin panel in the door.

"All that talk about eating and you've left half your food on your plate. Are you feeling alright?"

"Sure!" Kelly assured her friend. She forked a chunk of pineapple and popped it into her mouth to prove her point. "I've been so busy the past weeks that food has not been foremost on my mind. Everything tastes like it's had one coat of paint or been pasted, although you'd never know I've lost my appetite from the way these jeans are cutting me in half," she snickered, before changing the subject. "I think I'll put that little cupboard in the downstairs powder room by the utility area. It's kind of rustic."

"Are you on the pill?"

"What pill?" Kelly asked, picturing the cupboard hanging over the pine towel racks. At her friend's patient silence, she dismissed the cabinet and concentrated on what Susie had said, her face registering the implication. "Oh, that pill!"

"Yes, that pill!" Susie chided.

Kelly shook her head and frowned as she began some mental calculations. Time had gone by so quickly that she had not missed her feminine inconvenience. Blood rushed to her face as she realized it had been more than two months. "Oh, my goodness!"

Her startled exclamation made Susie burst into laughter. "Shall we go back and look for some nursery furnishings?"

"Susie, this is no laughing matter!" Kelly reproached, her hand going to her stomach as disbelief registered on her face.

She hadn't been prepared for a honeymoon because she hadn't known she was getting married. Then, everything happened so naturally the thought had never crossed her mind . . . and, obviously, had not crossed her husband's either.

The doctor confirmed her pregnancy the following week. Kelly kept her suspicions to herself, fighting the overwhelming urge to tell Mac. After all, her symptoms could have been a result of the unusual stress she had had to face of late—a surprise marriage, the discovery and death of her real father, and moving into a new home and decorating it.

But she did tell Teresa. It was the only way to get the housekeeper out of the house for the special dinner Kelly wanted to prepare for her husband. She wanted to make the evening special and very private when she told him that his child would be born in another six months. Teresa had cried with joy and then became smug as she pointed out the virtues of motherhood over flying . . . and for once, Kelly was not inclined to argue.

With Teresa happily off for a night of bingo or "beengo" as the woman called it, Kelly unpacked the wine and put it in the refrigerator to chill while she began to prepare the marinade for the beef she was going to serve over fried rice with stir-fried vegetables. Her nerves were taut as she cut up the Chinese cabbage and broccoli, wondering how Mac would react. Some men did not like children. She recalled the statement he had made when she had behaved so badly on their wedding night about not having had much experience with them.

Her hand jerked as the phone rang, jamming the point of the knife into her finger. Sucking the wound automatically, she reached for the receiver to answer the call.

"Hello, Kelly? This is Midge." At her acknowledgment, Mac's secretary went on. "Mac asked me to tell you that he wouldn't be home tonight.

He had to fly to Dallas over a snag in the Equipment-Aire contract and he'll be back tomorrow morning.''

Kelly's loud groan of disappointment set Midge into a defensive dissertation of how long Mac had been working on the contract and how important it was for the company to reach an agreement with the stubborn Peters family. It became so lengthy that a small seed of doubt began to sprout in the back of her mind even as she convinced Midge that she understood completely and hung up the phone. She did understand, Kelly thought insistently, as she put the beef and vegetables away. Her lips thinned. But she didn't have to like it.

TEN

"Citation two-seven-four requesting clearance for landing."

"Go ahead two-seven-four, nobody's up today."

The controller gave Kelly a wink as he put the mike down to watch the circling aircraft come in for an approach. Not being able to stay in bed a moment longer that morning, she had come in early with some biscuit sandwiches and shared breakfast with the Tower crew, her treat.

Her first night without Mac had been a restless one. It was amazing how quickly she had become accustomed to sleeping in his arms and the vacant pillow beside her had plagued her all night long. She watched the digital clock slowly turn its numbers until daybreak.

"I'm going on down to meet him," she told the guys, taking up her purse and slinging it over her shoulder.

"He'll probably lay another lip smacker on her like the first time they met," Pete Snyder joked with his fellow Tower mates.

"Maybe," Kelly acknowledged cheerily on her way down the stairs.

The steps dropped down from the side of the aircraft as Kelly sauntered toward it, her yellow sundress reflecting her mood at the prospect of seeing her husband. As silly as it seemed, she had really missed him; but the beef was still marinating and the plans were reset for the evening. His being away from time to time would be something she would have to get used to. She'd reminded herself of that fact all night long.

"Mac!" she called out, stepping up her pace as he emerged from the plane.

He wore khaki jeans that hugged muscular thighs and a brightly-colored shirt she had bought him in Mexico, making him appear quite the tourist. Waving, he flashed a white smile and turned back toward the entrance.

Kelly slowed as she saw Monica Peters emerge, grasping his arm as he helped her down the ramp. She, too, was dressed casually in a snug-fitting pair of white shorts that showed off her tanned legs to perfection and a sleeveless cotton sweater fitted to her curves. She clung to Mac until she was on solid ground, daring to release one arm to wave at Kelly.

It's not what it looks like, Kelly told herself firmly. Mac had to go to Dallas on business. She was certain of it. Monica had flown back with Uncle Dan before during business transactions between the two companies and it had meant nothing. Mac loved her, Kelly reasoned against the ugly jealousy that was taking root against her will.

"Oh look, darling. Your little bride is riding herd on you," Monica purred with a sly smile the same shade as her hot-pink sweater.

Reason be damned! Surely he could see what she was, Kelly fumed, trying hard to swallow her ire.

"Kelly, I didn't expect you to come down here," Mac said, ignoring Monica's comment and kissing Kelly lightly on the cheek. "Did you get my message?"

"About last night?" Kelly asked, disappointed at the briskness of the greeting.

"No, about the dinner party tonight. I called Teresa before we left Dallas, but you weren't home."

Kelly looked blank. "Dinner party?"

"Mac and I finally agreed," Monica interrupted. "But then we always do manage to work things out in spite of . . . complications. She slipped her hand through his arm and smiled. "At any rate, he invited me to see your new home and insisted on throwing a small party in celebration of our new contract. He's told me so much about it, I just can't wait to see it."

How could he do this to her, Kelly declared silently with a blue flash of irritation she could not disguise. It was bad enough to have the special evening put off again, but to have his ex-lover under the same roof!

"Monica, how about if you go on inside. Kelly and I will be along."

Monica glanced from Mac to Kelly with a speculative gleam. "Of course, darling. I'll check out the little girl's room and be waiting." The provocative swing of her hips as she retreated drew more than one appreciative look from the men unloading the luggage and print cases.

"Well, darling?" Kelly drawled in a perfect imitation of the dark-haired woman. There was no humor in her eyes.

Mac grinned. "Your claws are showing, love."

Kelly opened her mouth to retort and thought better of it. Instead, she pressed her lips into a thin line and waited for an explanation.

"Richard Peters and I just closed the deal for another twelve aircraft to be modified within a three-month period. It's been a battle of wills, but I think we both won." He slipped his arm around her shoulders and started to walk toward the terminal. "He's flying in this afternoon for a little celebration. The prototype is right this time. Midge is taking care of the catering and Teresa said the house was no problem. I wanted to show off my beautiful wife and the perfect job she has done in decorating our home."

"Flattery is helping," Kelly admitted, one corner of her mouth tilting upward. "I just had a special evening planned."

Mac stopped, turning her to face him. "They're all special with you, my pouting pretty."

His hands locked behind her, drawing her closer as his mouth devoured the softness of her lips. Her fingers crept up into the black hair that touched his collar as she molded against him in ready response. This is what she needed—his touch, his reassurance. It strengthened her. At that moment Kelly felt she could face anything the night held in store . . . as long as Mac was by her side.

The impromptu dinner party kept both Mac and Kelly busy the better part of the afternoon. The wet bar on the patio had to be stocked and the glasses needed to be unpacked and washed. It became fun, working side by side with her husband while Teresa concentrated on organizing the kitchen for the caterers. Midge had even arranged for a three-piece combo which set up in the corner of the living room so that the music might drift through the French doors to the deck that ran the full length of the house in the back and overlooked a sloping, shaded yard to a small creek.

Kelly never mentioned her secret, preferring to wait until she and Mac had a chance to be alone, which she realized as she hurriedly showered and dressed would be after the party. She chose a vermilion embroidered skirt Mac had purchased for her in Mexico and an off-the-shoulder blouse with the same artistic stitches on the ruffles. A pair of beaded sandals completed the effect.

She was not extremely uncomfortable after the guests arrived, in spite of the fact that the dinner party had grown to an open house. In the errands Mac had run that afternoon, he had invited almost everyone he saw. With the exception of Richard Peters and his daughter, Kelly had worked with most of them. Giles Courtney, the company attorney, Doug and Susie, Midge and her husband, Ken Hudson and his junior engineers were among those she was most familiar with. Everyone seemed equally pleased that the two companies had come to an agreement. The first order was just the beginning of production for the new line Equipment-Aire was going to offer, so the promise of future profits was another cause to celebrate.

"I just love what you've done with the house," Midge complimented Kelly as they left the dining room where a cold buffet had been set up, the caterer having coped beautifully with the unexpected increase in the guest list.

"Thanks, Midge. I love the job you did picking it out . . . and Susie," Kelly added, seeing her friend bristle with feigned insult.

"Hasn't she just surprised us all," Monica complimented with a hint of irony in her voice. Her lashes dipped as she looked around the room, resting her gaze briefly where Mac and her father were involved in conversation. "I'd rather expected to find something similar to that tasteless club with the airplane hanging in the middle of it.''

"Well, she hasn't surprised Mac. I think he knew from the first time he saw her that she was the only one for him,'' Midge said sweetly, coming to Kelly's defense. "He started right away finding out everything there was to find out about her . . . and wouldn't have another pilot. 'Change the schedule,' he'd say, and then grin like some moonstruck schoolboy.''

"Really?'' Kelly asked in surprise.

"Darling, that naive bit might fool men, but we can do without it. Oh, damn!'' Monica swore, jumping back as the martini Teresa was serving her slipped off the tray and into her lap.

"Oh, Senorita Peters, lo siento!'' Teresa exclaimed in horror, dabbing at the spreading dark spot on Monica's pale-blue sundress.

"Get away from me, you babbling idiot!'' Monica hissed, slapping the towel out of Teresa's hand.

Kelly put down the ginger ale she was sipping to settle her queasy stomach down and patted Teresa on the shoulder gently. "It's alright, Teresa. You clean this up and I'll help Miss Peters change,'' she said calmly, feeling sorry for the housekeeper until she detected a slight gleam in the dark eyes that made her wonder if it had been an accident.

"I'd appreciate that, Kelly,'' Monica flipped

over her shoulder before storming out of the room as if that were the least her hostess could do.

With a roll of her eyes heavenward for Susie's and Midge's benefit, Kelly followed. Monica had been peevish all evening. When the men had moved off to themselves, as men tended to do when business was the main topic of discussion, she had been dismissed by her father to join the women.

Monica was jerking her dress over her head when Kelly knocked gently and entered the room at her bidding. As the woman stomped over to the closet, Kelly picked up the discarded dress and folded it neatly.

"I'll have this cleaned for you, Monica. Poor Teresa is terribly upset."

"I'll bet she is!" Monica snapped, flashing green fire from across the room. "The old bat has always hated me. I told Mac he should have fed her to the sharks off that little beach of his."

Kelly stiffened, using great resolve to keep a smile on her face. "You've been to Villa Bianca?" she asked, as if making polite conversation.

At Monica's affirmation, some of the magic faded from her memory of the place. Of course, it was foolish to assume Mac had kept that place especially for her. It had been in his family for years. Yet, he had made her feel like it was all just for her.

'Surely, you don't think you're much different

than the other women he's taken there!" Monica taunted sarcastically.

Kelly flushed, forgetting her resolve to be polite. "I think so, Monica. He married me," she reminded her.

Green eyes narrowed maliciously. "Marriage is a small price to pay for fifty-percent of a company . . . and knowing you, you dangled your virginity as a prize to boot. Mac always was one for a challenge."

"That's a horrible thing to say! I can't believe anyone can be so . . . so . . ."

"Bitchy?" Monica laughed. But there was no amusement in her eyes. "Well, I am, darling . . . and Mac is my male counterpart. That's why we get on so well between flings with others. We couldn't stand to be married to each other, but we can't stay away permanently."

Kelly clenched her teeth until they ached, speaking through them in warning. "That is a lie and an insult to my husband!"

"My God, you are naive!" the other woman remarked in astonishment. "You just heard Midge say how he made it a point to find out everything about you . . . and you must admit, you had a rather whirlwind courtship."

There had been no courtship, Kelly was reminded. She hadn't even known about the wedding. Dear God, what would Monica think if she knew about that? Kelly's eyes raised hesitantly.

With an exaggerated sigh one might give a

child, Monica turned back to the closet and chose a form-fitting cotton dress. Its strapless bustier top required two to get it zipped. As Kelly grudgingly helped her, she met Monica's smug smile in the mirror and thinned her lips. The jade green of the garment that forced Monica's abundant cleavage to a focal point only served to deepen the green of her cat-like eyes. Monica was the epitome of exotic sophistication and elegance.

"Do you like this?"

Kelly grasped for her composure. If Mac ever allowed this woman in their home again, she vowed, she would move out. "Green looks lovely on you, Monica. If we are being candid, I think you know it."

"Mac bought this for me in Dallas. He said it brought out the color of my eyes and accentuates my tiny waist. He can span it with his hands . . . very talented hands," she purred, watching Kelly closely for a reaction as she touched up her fuschia lipstick.

"That was before we were married, Monica," Kelly said with forced patience. "And he couldn't have married me for my stock because I didn't even know I was going to inherit it. And, as for my . . . my inexperience, that is none of your business. This might be hard for someone like you to understand, but my husband and I love each other. That's an emotion I doubt you can relate to. As to why you are flaunting your past relationship before me, I have no idea, but it won't work."

Kelly's eyes went inadvertently to the manicured hands at the fragile waist. In a few months, her own would be swollen with Mac's child. How often she had seen pregnant women waddling clumsily about. Mac would be lucky to get his arms around her, let alone his hands.

"You don't have a ring."

"A ring is a worthless piece of jewelry," Kelly quoted her ex-fiance. "It's what's in here," she said, placing her hand over her heart, "That counts."

"It can also be a drag . . . a reminder of a commitment one doesn't take that seriously. A man on the make, certainly doesn't want a gold band scaring off any good prospects. I admit that when any of my escorts wear one it hampers my style . . . a little." At Kelly's strained silence, Monica went on. "And as for your stock, Mac did know. He wanted to buy all of it, but Dan Mooney explained that half was to be yours."

"No!" Kelly objected, her fingers drawing into a fist.

"If you don't believe me, ask Giles. He drew up the contracts and the will. He was involved in the negotiations. Or better yet, ask Mac," Monica challenged as she walked past Kelly and stopped to smooth her skirt at the door. "And if you think Mac has forgotten me, just keep watch."

It couldn't be, Kelly told herself as she stepped

out into the dimly-lit corridor. Monica's retreating head disappeared down the steps. The woman was a vicious bitch who just wanted to make her miserable. She had always treated her like that over Ken, and now it was Mac.

The dancing had begun when Kelly rejoined the group. She moved numbly through the crowd, smiling and returning appropriate comments as she made her way to the bar. Teresa had taken her half-finished drink, so she ordered another from the white-jacketed bartender.

Her eyes found Mac and, predictably, Monica at the terrace door, speaking to Ken Hudson and Richard Peters. Monica was the center of attention as she lavished praise on Mac for his lovely home.

"I see you still have that hot-tempered Mexican maid. I'm surprised Kelly hasn't run her out by now," Kelly heard Monica say as she joined them.

"Kelly doesn't seem to have any trouble with Teresa. Do you, love?"

Kelly shook her head. "None. She's like a dear mother hen. I don't know what I'd do without her."

As if she sensed she was being discussed, Teresa looked up from the table she was clearing across the room and smiled as she saw her employer slip his arm around his wife. Kelly caught her eye and returned it, moving her head from side to side slightly in answer to the silent

question the Mexican cook asked, letting her know
that Don Jaime did not know yet about the baby.

"Mac, darling, do you remember this old dress?
I was telling Kelly about that trip."

Kelly's smile faded as she glanced nervously at
her husband. He laughed, the corners of his mouth
drawing up to form dimples she had kissed on
more than one occasion, as he gave Monica an
appreciative sweep with his eyes.

"I don't think I'll ever forget it. That was the
week you joined us at the country club after that
tournament. Remember, Richard?"

"Damned right. I've never been so wet in my
life. You two got off lucky!" Richard Peters's
boisterous laughter rivaled the speakers in front of
the band. "Damned cart left me stranded on the
tenth hole in the middle of the damnedest storm I
ever hope to see."

"Excuse me, Mac, but since you three are obviously reminiscing, would you mind if I asked your
lovely wife to dance?" Ken Hudson intervened,
his eyes meeting the suddenly alert grey ones.

"That's up to the lady," Mac answered gra-
ciously, giving Kelly an extra squeeze before she
stepped forward to take Ken's offer.

It wasn't until she was in his arms on the terrace
among the other dancing couples that she realized
she was trembling. She didn't want to dance. She
wanted to just get away from everyone so that she
could reason things out. She wasn't normally this

emotional. Where were the nerves of steel that belonged to the Valkyrie?

"You don't look well, sweetheart. Something you ate or something you heard?" Ken asked perceptively.

Kelly raised her face to meet Ken's inquiring brown eyes. She couldn't speak. Her bottom lip quivered and his image became so blurred that she had to look away.

Ken's embrace tightened in spite of the fact that they were well within view of her husband. He turned her so that his back protected her. "What has the bastard done, Kelly?"

"Monica," she managed brokenly. An overwhelming wave of nausea accompanied the name and she clung to Ken for support as her knees threatened to give way. "Oh God, I'm going to be sick," she whispered desperately.

The trees above them whirled as she felt Ken's supporting arms help her down the steps to the lawn. Her skin was clammy as she eased down on a white wrought iron bench in the shadow of the terrace. She felt the cool, dry touch of his handkerchief as he wiped her forehead gently. Weakly, she leaned against him as the nausea began to recede. Her shoulders shook gently and tears spilled against his knit shirt.

"She . . . she said Mac only married me for my stock . . . and he couldn't have known."

"Kelly," Ken chided, his hand rubbing her bare shoulder reassuringly. "As a man, I can tell you

Monica is lying. She's just jealous. Hell, she's tried to hook Mac since she broke him and his first wife up.''

"Ken!"

Ken swore silently at his slip of the tongue. "Look, I have no reason to defend the guy. He took what I wanted . . . still want," he admitted softly, one finger tracing the delicate taper of her face. "But, he loves you, Ace. He doesn't take his eyes off you. I've watched him watch you all evening and I'd bet money that is why Monica is outdoing herself at being a bitch. She's outclassed and she knows it." He chuckled suddenly. "I can't believe I'm saying this . . . and risking my job and possibly bodily harm to do it."

At this, Kelly mustered a faltering smile. "Mac wouldn't do anything," she assured him, recalling Mac's conversation after he had found her and Ken in his office. "I needed this, Ken. Thank you so much."

Kelly took his hands as he pulled her to her feet and hugged him affectionately. She took a deep breath, turning to go back up the steps, and held it as she met the frosty stare of her husband. A chill swept over her, causing her to shudder involuntarily.

"Susie said that you looked ill, so I promised to check on you. She didn't say, however, that you were already in good hands. If you're alright, I'll go on back to our guests."

The indifference in his voice was like a slap in

the face. Perhaps the reflection of the light had given the now impenetrable grey eyes that cold glint. Mac seemed no more upset that she was alone in the shadows with her ex-fiance than he had been when he walked in on Ken's affectionate kiss.

"I'm fine, Mac. I just needed some fresh air," she answered quietly.

With a curt nod of his head, he disappeared, leaving her alone again with Ken. Slowly, Kelly exhaled.

"You see? I told you he wouldn't do anything."

She hid her hurt so well that Ken never noticed as they rejoined the party. Her smile became fixed as she circulated, going through the motions of being the perfect hostess. After midnight the guests began to dwindle in numbers. The combo packed up their equipment and left. Only Doug, Richard Peters, and Mac remained, engaged in a conversation about the conversion of the engine in the new model, Ken having left shortly after eleven with Midge and her husband. Monica sat on the arm of Mac's chair, clinging to his every word as if fascinated.

"How about if I help clean up," Susie offered brightly. "They'll talk pistons and turbo stuff all night."

Kelly gave a wan smile. "Thanks."

She picked up a tray of hors d'oeuvres and carried it into the kitchen where Teresa was ordering the caterers about like a queen in her domain.

"No, no, no!" Teresa objected as she saw Kelly put the tray on the counter by the sink. "You no clean up! You be hostess!"

"There's no one to hostess, Teresa," Kelly informed her.

Susie came through the door, four glasses of varying fullness precariously gathered in each hand. "Where do these go?"

"Hostess her!" Teresa commanded, sliding a tray under the glasses to avoid a disaster.

The ache in Kelly's temples made it too difficult to argue. Massaging them gently, she turned to her friend. "Want some coffee?"

"What's up between you and Mac?" Susie asked, answering her by helping herself to a cup and pouring one for Kelly as well. "Did you tell him?"

"No, and why?" Kelly asked, dropping onto one of the barstools in the midst of the cleanup confusion.

Susie shrugged. "I don't know . . . just bad vibes maybe. He came in from the terrace with a face like thunder. I half-expected lightning to strike from those grey eyes of his."

"Well, you sent him to look for me!" Kelly chided, more pleased than disturbed at Susie's news. He had cared. He was just doing as he had mentioned, working around Ken to save him.

"Here, you take these," Teresa interrupted them shoving two aspirin at Kelly.

Kelly declined because of the baby. She just couldn't pull her wits together. Her mind was clouded with doubts that fatigue permitted to run rampant. A good night's rest in her husband's arms would be all she needed to restore her, physically and emotionally.

"So, what happened?" Susie asked eagerly as Teresa shuffled off, barking at one of the uniformed men carrying out trash.

Kelly gave her a brief account of what Monica had said, how Ken had restored her confused thoughts, and the awkward situation Mac had found them in.

"Well, Ken ought to know. After all, he's had a time or two with the hussy, too," Susie pointed out.

"He was very sweet. I really . . ." Kelly yawned, covering her mouth with her hand politely. "I'm sorry," she chuckled softly. "I just don't have my usual get up and go."

"Then go to bed. You have your condition to consider," Susie insisted. "And I am going to drag my husband away so that you can have your sleep."

"You're a doll."

Susie did exactly what she promised. She literally walked up to Doug, took his arm, and hauled him out of his seat. After a polite thank you to Mac and Kelly and a good-bye to the Peters, she dragged him toward the door as he voiced his opinion on the TBO, or time before overhaul, of the engine they were installing in the Equipment-Aire planes. Mac stood with his arm around Kelly and waved at the departing couple. When their tail lights were fading down the street, he closed the door.

"I think I'm going to go on upstairs, if you don't mind," Kelly informed him. "I'm exhausted."

The way he stared at her left her unsettled. It was as if he were trying to see beyond her pale face, into the depths of blue that returned his gaze evenly.

"I'll extend your excuses to our guests and be right up as soon as they are settled. I have to take them to the field at seven, so it shouldn't be much longer . . . and I want to talk to you."

"That makes two of us," Kelly grinned, covering the uncertainty that flourished under his scrutiny. She stepped up on tiptoe and planted a kiss on the end of his nose. "I'll be waiting. Wake me if I fall asleep," she added impishly, flicking a piece of imaginary lint from his casual cotton jacket.

The fact that Mac had not responded in kind, brought a frown to her face as she lay in the middle of the huge bed. He had no need to be jealous. She loved him more than she ever dreamed it possible to love someone. Her hand went to her stomach in a caressing motion. And she loved the fact

that she was going to have his baby. Kelly glanced
at the clock anxiously. One-thirty. Well, she'd just
rest her eyes until he came up. He'd said he'd
wake her.

ELEVEN

The clock said seven-thirty when Kelly shook herself from the stupor of her sleep and realized she had missed Mac—not only that morning, but the night before as well. The covers on his side of the bed were still neatly folded back as she had left them. It didn't take her long to don jeans and a shirt to go to the plant, her mind still dwelling on the question that had haunted her sleep all night. Had he known about the stock or was Monica counting on her lacking the courage to confront him in order to find out the truth?

And where had he been all night? That question tied her stomach in knots as she rushed out in the hall toward the gracefully winding steps. At the landing, she saw Teresa coming out of the guest room Monica had used. Kelly would have merely spoken and gone on her way had the housekeeper not started at the sight of her and suspiciously shoved something into the laundry basket in the hall. Not wanting to know, and yet having to, Kelly went up to the basket and took out Mac's jacket in spite of Teresa's pitiful plea not to.

The sickening feeling she had felt the night before rose again as she drove through the gate to Custom Aero, not bothering to wave at the gate-keeper. Kelly tried not to believe Mac had spent the night in his ex-lover's room, but the evidence had been there. Everything Monica had said fit. Hadn't he recognized the jade dress, and pleasantly, too.

A razor-sharp constriction in her throat kept her from speaking to the members of the skeleton shift that worked on the weekends as she walked with determination down the waxed corridor toward Mac's office. In their own home, she moaned silently. That was what added insult to injury. He'd brought Monica to their home and slept with her. And Kelly had been just like her mother . . . too blinded by her love to see what was really happening. But Mac was so much more accomplished than her stepfather, so much more polished.

Voices coming from the president's office slowed her step as she walked by Midge's desk, now vacant until Monday. The door was ajar and a light shafted through it. She could see their shadows, distorted, but definitely belonging to Monica and her husband. Numbly, Kelly stopped and listened, leaning against the desk for support.

''I can't tell you how much I enjoyed last

night," Monica was cooing, a shadowy arm reaching out to touch the lapel of Mac's jacket. "You went to so much trouble."

"It was worth it, Monica," Mac replied sarcastically. "And I think you know it. Now, I want to get back to Kelly before she wakes up, so let's get moving, shall we?"

"Touching . . . you certainly have her fooled. She thinks you are a saint, but I know better."

The two shadows came together and, as the conversation died, Kelly caught her breath and rushed out of the room. She couldn't bear to face him. She had wanted to, but not now, not with Monica's perfume still clinging to his shirt or her lipstick still coloring his lips.

She hardly realized where she was going except to get away. The doorways and exit signs were a blur as she passed them, choking on her tears. She bit her lip until it throbbed like her pulse. She would learn to hate him. She would not sit idly and let him destroy her as her mother permitted the man she loved to do to her.

"Hey, Ace, what's happening?" Mickey called out to her above the loud rock music he worked to as she stumbled into the hangar where her small Cessna was kept.

"Mickey, help me get my plane ready." A sob caught in her throat and she had to fight to regain control.

"What's wrong?" the young mechanic asked, his ever-present grin fading.

"I can't talk now. Please help me."

Mickey lifted his ball cap and scratched his head reluctantly. "Have you heard the weather?"

"No . . ." Kelly hesitated.

"There's a cold front coming in from the west. Kinda unstable for the present up there."

"I'll be careful," she assured him. "Now, let's get going."

Emotion set aside momentarily, Kelly began a methodical pre-flight check. Mickey was an excellent mechanic, always checking her plane out periodically, so Kelly had little qualms about the machine not giving its utmost. The young man opened the sliding doors of the hangar for Kelly to take the plane out, but upon seeing Mac helping Monica into the company Citation, she held back. Mickey looked at her curiously as she watched Mac go back to the Tower entrance, his familiar figure bringing fresh anguish to her heart.

"Mickey, be an angel and take her out for me. I have to make a call and then I'll be ready," she said suddenly.

She had to know . . . to hear it from Mac's own lips about the stock. Monica was an accomplished seductress. Perhaps Mac had had a little too much to drink and slipped. Perhaps . . . She just had to know, she thought singly, forcing the other knowledge out of her mind for the moment.

Her hand shook as she dialed the Tower extension and asked for Mac. In a moment, he came to the phone.

"Mac . . ." her voice caught and she swallowed the blade that cut her off.

"Kelly? Kelly, where are you? Teresa just called a few minutes ago . . ."

"Mac, did you know I was going to inherit Uncle Dan's stock before you married me?"

There was a brief pause before he spoke grimly, ignoring her question. "Where are you, Kelly?"

"Did you?" She backed against the wall, waiting.

"Kelly, we'll talk about it when I see you," he insisted. "What's that music?"

"Answer me now, Mac. Yes or no, will do."

"No, it won't. Are you in Mickey's bay?"

Kelly's voice hardened as her defenses began to erect a shell around her injured heart. "It doesn't matter, Mac. I guess you don't have to say."

She hung up the phone dejectedly and loped out to the plane where Mickey had the engine purring for action. Mac had guessed where she was and she didn't want to see him. She just wanted to get up in the sky alone to think.

"Keep tuned to the weather, Ace," Mickey cautioned as he turned the plane over to her. "Personally, I think you're nuts."

She was nuts, Kelly thought as she taxied toward an open runway and radioed the Tower for clearance. It ran against her grain to disregard mother nature.

"Hold up, Cessna seven-niner-zero. The boss man is on his way out."

Her indecision disappeared immediately. "Cessna seven-niner-zero taking the north runway. If there's anybody in my way, Pete, clear 'em," Kelly radioed back.

"Jesus, Kelly, hold on! Mac's on his way."

"I'm gone, Pete. I own half this company and I'll do as I damned well please."

Kelly ignored the protesting transmissions, turning them down as she concentrated on her takeoff. In the corner of her eye, she spotted a vehicle approaching the runway and realized Mac was trying to head her off. Well, he hadn't reckoned with her custom Lycoming. At half the distance between them, Kelly lifted off, the engine clawing powerfully toward the clouds overhead. In no time at all the crisscross of runways and tiny vehicles looked like a toy airport below.

It wasn't until she leveled off that her nerves began to get the best of her. Her brow was beaded with perspiration and her hands trembled at the controls. This was ridiculous. She prided herself on her flying and cool manner, but here she was on the verge of tears.

"Cessna seven-niner-zero, come in. Kelly, you're acting irrational. There's a pre-frontal squall line ahead of the cold front. Now, come back down! This isn't necessary."

Kelly ignored Mac's order, her chin jutting out squarely in defiance.

"It's dangerous, damn it!" The angry voice came across in frustration.

As if he really cared! Kelly grabbed the mike with a vengeful jerk. "Maybe your luck will hold out and the baby and I won't come back . . . then you can have all that precious stock to yourself!" she sobbed bitterly. "Monica was wrong in your office a while ago. I do know what a bastard you are!"

"Baby? What the . . ."

Kelly cut off the radio and blinked to clear her eyes in order to read the instruments. She would make a short flight to Houston and put down there. She could book a room in a hotel until the front moved through and decide whether or not to return to Corpus Christi. If she did, however, it would not be to Mac Mackenzie. She wondered what her chances of getting her old place back were.

Visibility was poor. Ahead cumulus clouds dotted the sky. Kelly turned on the weather station and ascended above the haze level, noting the increase in temperature. She might have to go east, further out of her way in order to avoid the squall line. The altimeter warned her the tops of the clouds were climbing, forcing her up with them.

A shiver ran the length of her spine when she saw the stretch of clouds ahead that rose higher than experience told her she could fly safely. The high peaks formed anvil tops that made her inhale deeply and let out her breath slowly to maintain her control. Just what Mac had said . . . a prefrontal line with a solid bulbous wall, varying from misty white to threatening rolling smoke in places.

Gradually, her professional training took over. Her eyes scanned the radar, searching for the storm cells that might tear the small Cessna apart. To fly above them was out; and she dared not drop below the rolling clouds for a torturous ride and zero visibility. What she needed to find was ahead somewhere . . . a saddle between the cells that might let her through. Eyes and radar worked in conjunction until Kelly spied a likely prospect. All she had to do was make it through before the clouds below rose to close it.

"Oh, God!" she prayed as she made the run, feeling the powerful updraft that made her fears a reality.

The smoky turmoil surrounded her. Her full mouth became set as she concentrated on her heading. All of the instructions came back to her— slow the engine to sixty percent above stall, keep the wings level, turn on all cockpit lights, and lower the seat. Methodically, she ran through the procedures of flying in the midst of a storm, flinching as a nearby bolt of lightning nearly blinded her in the formidable darkness. She could smell the ozone permeating the inside of the small plane and felt the small hairs at the base of her neck rise. Don't panic! The caution echoed repeatedly in her brain.

When the hail began it was deafening. Kelly grasped the controls, knuckles white. The plane jolted and jarred, heaved up and squashed down until she was dizzy. The radio squealed announcing the explosive boom and flash that followed. It would not have surprised her to see the wings torn off at any moment.

Keep calm, she told herself after what seemed to be hours of struggling to keep the plane stable. There was some comfort offered by the erratic voices on the VHF. It wasn't as bad as it had been at first. She was certain the ride was not quite as rough and the abusive hail had stopped.

The first ray of sunlight shafting through made her laugh in relief and then cry. At a lower altitude, she saw the waters of the Gulf and adjusted her course. She was going to put down at the first airfield she came to. One front was bad enough.

Flying in good visibility again, Kelly dropped over the waters, unwinding as she watched ships make their determined way across the blue surface, leaving a wispy vee of white that dissipated into blue again. The radio crackled, prompting her to tune in to a local frequency. At the same time, the steadfast purr of the engine ceased with a sputtering sound. Kelly immediately checked her instrument readings. The oil pressure was gone and the engine was red hot. Something must have gone wrong in the turbulance of the storm, she thought, eyes searching the shimmering blue ahead of her for one of the islands or bars that protected the Texas coastline.

"May Day, May Day," Kelly called out over

the emergency frequency. She thought she could bring the plane down on the island, but she needed her position noted.

An answer came across within seconds. With surprising calm, she gave her position and then flicked on the transponder as the comptroller prompted her to do. Now all she had to do was put down safely, something she had practiced time and time again without the power of an engine.

It was a rough landing. The sand was not the most ideal surface and the roll of the low dunes made it worse. The Cessna finally pitched forward with a resounding thud into a dune too high for the sinking wheels to handle. Kelly felt her shoulders jerked back by the harness that kept her from hitting the windshield. And then there was silence.

After a moment, she assessed her surroundings, her heart beating loudly in her ears above the static of the radio. Her plane was intact. Officials knew where she was. She had survived the storm front, more of an accomplishment than the forced landing. It was easy to practice forced landings, but storms were not sought out for instruction as a rule. Relief made her sink back against the seat weakly.

Stupid, the self-recriminations began. Mac was right. If she had had to leave, she should have kept to ground transportation. Now she was stranded on some coastal island. Well, you ought to have plenty of time to think, she chastised herself harshly.

Too uptight to dwell on her personal problems, Kelly climbed out of the aircraft. Her face paled as she saw the pitiful dented finish she had kept so meticulously polished. The hail had demolished it. Her battered plane looked like a reject from a junkyard. An apologetic groan escaped her lips as she rubbed her hand along the side of the aircraft as if to give her pet comfort from the horrible wounds.

The wind was blowing threateningly from the west, drawing Kelly's attention to the western horizon, dark with clouds. My God, not another one, she prayed. She crawled back inside the plane and tuned to a weather station. Houston was being hit now by the front. That meant it was only a few miles from her. What was it now, she wondered, as she tried to recall the simple way to gauge the distance from a storm. Count the seconds between the thunder and the flash and divide by five for each mile.

The black horizon flashed raggedly and twelve seconds later the answering rumble came. A little over two miles, she guessed. Anxiously Kelly looked around the island. The only protection she had was the Cessna. The narrow island was barren with the exception of the dried grass and sea oats.

Another transmission from the emergency station confirmed her suspicion. They were not sending any rescue craft out until the front passed, since she was relatively safe for the time being.

Kelly was instructed to maintain radio contact and stay in the plane until then.

Left with little alternative, she settled in the seat. The wind blowing in through the open hatch gave her scant relief from the humid heat. Her stomach growled, reminding her that she had not eaten since she had fixed a small plate from the buffet the night before. The half biscuit she'd tried to down that morning hardly counted.

After a thorough search, she found a package of cheese crackers and made them her lunch. As she ate them, she noted the sky darkening with the storm's approach. She tapped the instrument panel.

"Well, we made it this far, old girl. Another blow can't be so bad."

Later, she was to regret those words. The tide lashed up on the island, spraying the plane that rocked in the gusting winds. Eyes wide, Kelly curled up in the seat, helpless to do anything except pray that it would soon be over. She found herself wishing for strong comforting arms, but dismissed the inadvertent thought mournfully and clasped her hands over her belly.

"Oh, baby," she sniffed, the emotions she had managed to shelve during flight, creeping back to unnerve her. "You have a stupid mother and a bastard father . . . what chance do you stand?"

Kelly soon became accustomed to the shaking of the plane. She rested her head on her knees, shutting out the storm as she closed her eyelids.

The radio crackled reassuringly as it had before, soon becoming a snappy drone. It wasn't until a terrible explosion ripped the side of her plane, that she was startled from her seat.

Everything went into motion. Where the wing had been was a gaping hole. A vicious arm of wind and salt spray grasped the plane, flipping it over. Kelly, no longer in her seatbelt and shoulder harness, pitched helplessly inside the dark cockpit, crying out as her head hit the instrument panel. The pain that stabbed her brain was diverted as throttles jabbed at her ribs and other protruding objects attacked her in the kaleidoscope of chaos that made every nerve scream in agony. Then, blissfully, shock began its anesthetic flow through her bruised and bleeding body until the plane stilled and darkness enveloped her.

TWELVE

The cockpit was incredibly white, Kelly mused groggily as she tried to see through hazy eyes; except for those blue and green geometric curtains that seemed so far away. There were no curtains like that in her plane, a small voice objected. She started to close her eyes again because feeling was starting to come back with her consciousness and it hurt.

"Kelly? Kelly, honey, please wake up."

A familiar voice, that of a woman interfered. Now she was shaking her. My God, didn't she know how that hurt? Kelly protested with a groan. There. At least she was squeezing her hand now.

"Mrs. Mackenzie . . . Mrs. Mackenzie."

Cold hands touched her cheeks, making her shudder. They must belong to the strange voice calling her Mrs. Mackenzie, because her hand was still being squeezed. With a sigh of defeat, Kelly gave them their way and opened her eyes. She had never seen the woman leaning over her, holding her face. Kelly frowned, wincing as the ache in her head became more prominent.

"You're in the hospital, Mrs. Mackenzie," she was saying. She did have a kind face.

"Oh, thank God," the familiar voice sighed, drawing Kelly's attention to the figure that moved closer to the bed. "Kelly, it's me, Susie."

Of course, it was. What was the silly thinking? "Hi," Kelly managed, surprised at the effort it took.

"Do you remember what happened, Mrs. Mackenzie?"

Kelly looked back at the nurse and nodded. "The storm wrecked my plane on the ground." She recalled the terrible rush of wind and water and the pain as she tumbled around inside the catapulting cockpit like a limp doll. "Is anything broken?" She tried to assess her injuries, but it hurt too much to move.

The nurse shook her head with a patient smile. "You're just badly bruised, dear, and you have a concussion. The baby is fine."

The baby! Kelly closed her eyes, feeling so very foolish. For a moment, she had forgotten she was carrying Mac's child. Mac . . .

"Where's Mac, Susie?"

There was an uncomfortable look on Susie's face that pained her more than the aches that were springing to life all over her body. He wasn't there. He hadn't even cared enough to see how she was.

"I'll go call him right now."

"No!" Kelly protested, her fingers clasping the hands that held hers.

"We have to call your husband, Mrs. Mackenzie," the nurse informed her in a clinical tone. "However, the doctor said that you do not have to see him if you do not wish to."

"When can I leave?" If Mac couldn't be troubled to stay with her, then she certainly didn't want to see him.

"The doctor wants you here a few days for observation . . . just to make sure there will be no complications from the concussion or with the pregnancy." The nurse looked across Kelly at Susie. "I'll call Mr. Mackenzie and let him know his wife has regained consciousness."

The doctor came in and after several questions, gave her a thorough examination. Afterward, Kelly collapsed on the pillow, fully cognizant that every joint in her body functioned, painfully so. She had wanted to talk to Susie, who had stepped out in the corridor during the exam, but sleep claimed her before the doctor finished telling her the extent of her injuries.

Kelly lost track of time. There was little difference in day and night. The staff was always bright-eyed and smiling. The curtain shut out the daylight. Flowers came in daily. Susie came at odd hours, walking with her through the corridors as she regained her strength. But Mac never showed his face. A large vase of roses arrived from him daily, each day a different color, but he did not come personally. Each arrangement was signed, "Love, Mac."

As her body healed, her state of mind became more desolate.

It was over. Unlike the girl in the fairy tale, she would not live happily ever after. Mac did not want to make up. He'd done his duty by providing Susie with a hotel room near the hospital in order to see to any needs Kelly might have.

Susie was helpful, but her reluctance to discuss Mac only confirmed Kelly's suspicions. It was her eyes that betrayed her. There was pity in them, coupled with concern. Her friend knew of Mac's intentions and did not have the heart to tell her. Susie's conversations dwelled on what was happening at the plant with Doug and how well Kelly was progressing.

The day Kelly was discharged from the hospital, a private flight was chartered from Houston to Corpus Christi. She had decided to return to their home only to pack her belongings and to hear from her husband what he had been trying to tell her with his absence.

Some arrangements for her future had already been made from her hospital room. Since she had done some renovating, Mrs. Brooks had not rented her apartment yet and promised to hold it for her. A brief call from the hospital to Giles Courtney authorized him to send the landlady the advance on the rent. Once she was up to it, Kelly would find another attorney. It was awkward, as Giles had pointed out, to represent both Mac and her.

Kelly fastened her seatbelt, her nerves on edge as the Citation turbojet took off from the metropolitan airport. She didn't bother to watch it grow smaller or try to recognize familiar landmarks as she usually did. Her mind was on her impending meeting with her husband.

As much as she knew, as much as she had been hurt by that knowledge, Kelly still could not bring herself to hate him. His absence only served to increase her longing to be held and comforted by him once more. Yet, she knew what she must face and tried to mentally prepare herself. She would not mention the termination of the marriage. He could at least have the courage to do that.

She reclined the seat, her body engulfed in tides of weariness and despair. Gently, she folded her hands across her lap. There was the one consolation. She would at least have the baby.

The gravitational force that pressed her against the back of her cushioned seat woke her as the flaps were adjusted on the wings to make up for wind variation in the landing. Kelly glanced out the window curiously but her eyes went past the wing to the familiar runway. Spanish signs identified the gates and various affiliated buildings. Merida!

She kept her seatbelt fastened as the plane

turned at the end of the runway and taxied to the terminal. The pilot had been on the plane when she came aboard. His identity had not crossed her mind at the time. She had assumed it was one of the corporate pilots, but now there was no doubt as to the identity of the man flying the plane.

Of course, she thought bitterly. A few well-tipped clerks and a divorce could be as easily attained as a marriage. When the plane stopped, Kelly unfastened the belt and rose from her seat. She was smoothing the wrinkles from her skirt as Mac emerged from the cockpit.

For a moment neither of them spoke. Kelly stood stiffly, returning the contemplative appraisal. She was neither prepared for what she saw, nor anticipating the effect his physical presence had on her. He looked haggard and tired. His lean square features were gaunt and dark circles hung under the grey eyes that met hers. There was an overwhelming urge to go to him, to kiss the circles and seek the warmth of his body against hers. It was so overpowering that she sank back to her seat in an attempt to regain her composure.

It was not going to be easy. All the scenes she had rehearsed were useless. It was one thing to deal with Mac in her mind and quite another to stand face-to-face with him.

"I have your papers. If you will, just sit tight and I'll be back as soon as I can."

Kelly frowned. "Where are we going?"

"Home," came the husky answer that drifted back to her as he left the plane.

It was just as well that she was seated, for the blood drained from her face, taking her strength with it. Home. Was this his idea of a cruel joke, she screamed silently. She didn't want those precious memories of Villa Bianca tarnished any more than Monica had already done. Did he think her so weak that she needed to have the final word broken to her gently or did he plan an ironic announcement on the beach where he had first taken her.

Again the rehearsals started as her defenses reinforced her composure. Her planned speeches became repetitive, her reactions not what she would have. She wanted to accept it gracefully in mutual agreement, not fall apart in a fit of tears.

The authorities inspected their plane briefly, identifying Kelly at the same time as the girl on the passport, and promptly sent them on their way to Tulum. On the boat ride, Kelly remained seated, her arms folded on the rail as she stared blankly at the passing water. Her stomach was slightly tremulous at the smell of the diesel fumes from the engine, but the wind changed enough to grant her sufficient reprieve. Occasionally, she was aware of grey eyes watching her intently, but Mac never offered to join her; which was just as well, considering his effect on her nerves.

Her features remained schooled in an aloof manner until she saw the familiar figure of Teresa shuffling hurriedly down the steps to the white dock to meet them. By the time Kelly was in the wiry arms that crushed her tender ribs, she was in tears. She couldn't help herself. All the misery of the days in Houston, the finality of her visit drained her eyes until her ragged sobs were hoarse and dry.

She ached all over, the center of her pain, her heart. Teresa helped her to the room she and Mac had shared and placed cold cloths over her swollen red eyes to soothe them, all the time speaking in a soft coaxing Spanish that, in spite of its foreign sound, offered comfort.

At twilight, Kelly dressed in an outfit Teresa had brought for her, chosen from the closet that only held feminine clothing. Her traveling dress ruined from her rest, she donned a fresh linen sundress with scooped bodice, embroidered in warm oranges and yellows against an off-white background. She had no appetite, but she supposed that supper was to be the dread occasion.

Mac seated her next to him, and took his customary place at the head of the table. His conversation was polite, nothing more, nothing less. She assured him she felt quite recovered from the accident. It was indeed a lovely evening with the breeze coming in off the water. No, she did not want any wine, the only reference to their baby being made in a short acknowledgment of grey eyes dropping to the wide straw belt at her waist.

Kelly could not bring herself to eat. The more

she chewed, the harder her food became to swallow. Great swallows of ginger ale helped wash what little she consumed down. She moved the spiced shrimp around on her plate, cutting them up and mixing them with the vegetables and rice until it looked like a scramble of table scraps.

Why didn't he just come out and say it, she wondered, as Teresa took up the dessert plates, looking mournfully at the cake Kelly had mutilated. Or was he waiting until they were alone.

"Are you up to a walk?"

Kelly nodded, gooseflesh rising on her arms in apprehension. His touch burned her as he brushed her skin with his hands.

"Do you need a wrap?"

He was so damned polite, it was maddening!

"No, I'm fine, thank you," she lied flatly.

Her world was about to come to an end, her life as well. Her body would go through the motions of living, but her heart could not survive this. She had taken their marriage seriously. She had given him her all. There would be no love left for anyone except the baby. After all these years, she finally understood her mother; but Kelly would not find solace in the bottle. She would find it in her child.

The moon-glazed sea looked like a silvered mirror that rippled endlessly toward the starlit horizon. The beach glowed, white sand against grey-black limestone as they meandered down the carved steps toward it. Kelly's heart set a rapid pace, growing larger with each beat until her breathing labored. Mac's arm, lightly resting at her waist, should she slip, sent hot and cold flashes to every nerve center until her body shrieked in frustration.

"You're not feeling well, are you?" he asked, as her sandals sunk in the night-cooled sand.

A hand caressed the side of her cheek, casting a tormented light to the sapphire of her eyes. His brow furrowed and the hand dropped.

"I'll take you back. I'm rushing you," he said, fixing her hand on the arm he offered for polite escort.

It hurt her. The way he looked at her, eyes devoid of emotion. The distant way he treated her, as if she were a stranger instead of his wife, even if soon to be ex-wife.

"No, you're not damn you!" she blurted out, tearing away from him. "Just go ahead and say it and get it over with. I . . . I can't stand this any more!" She choked on her tears. "It was better when you weren't around!"

His face might have been made of the same stone as the steps as he moved toward her, seizing her arms. "Was it, Kelly?" His voice was strained, as the distance between their lips became a breath and no more. "Permit me to find out for myself," he demanded, taking her mouth completely with his own.

Kelly could not fight him. Cursing him for his cruelty, she gave him his satisfaction, responding with the long denied want of their separation. He would use it against her, but to this assault there was no defense. She tasted her own tears as he gently brushed her lips once more before leaving the searing imprint of his own on them to cool with their separation.

"Why are you dragging this out, Mac? I'll give you what you want. Just let me and the baby be!" she cried, hysteria creeping into her voice.

"Dragging what out, Kelly?" he asked, the prison of his arms holding her captive.

"The divorce!"

The word came out with a dizzying blow, making her swoon against him. Her hands clawed their way up his arms for support in spite of the steel band that held her securely.

"Kelly!" he called out in alarm, sweeping her up into his arms.

He carried her to the steps and sat down, holding her in his lap like a cradled child. She sobbed incoherently against the thin material of his shirt in humiliation and defeat.

"Is that what you want?" He pried her face away, holding it so that he could see it. "Will you convict me of adultery and marrying you for your money without hearing me out? Damn you, Kelly, if I weren't scared to death I'd hurt you and the baby, I'd shake you!" Instead, he clutched her to him again roughly, his body trembling with frustrated rage as he went on. "You have no idea what it was like not knowing where you were or what had happened . . . and then finding you half-conscious in what was left of your plane. I died a thousand deaths, you little idiot!''

"You didn't even bother to see how I was," Kelly retorted bitterly through ragged breaths.

"After the way you flew into me at the wreak-age, the doctor was afraid my presence might hinder your recovery . . . that you might lose the baby. Susie wasn't even supposed to talk about me.''

"What?'' Kelly looked at the face only inches away in confusion. There were several times she had asked for Mac, only to have her best friend divert the direction of the conversation; but Kelly had assumed Susie was protecting her from Mac's lack of concern.

"You expressed your displeasure with me in explicit terms with such vehemence that the doctor had to sedate you to get you in the helicopter.'' He added reproachfully, "I was not the most popular man on the rescue team.''

Kelly shook her head in denial. She remembered nothing of her rescue.

"You gave Ken Hudson hell for jumping to conclusions, for thinking the worse, but at least he had the guts to go to you about it, instead of charging off half-cocked in the middle of a storm front!''

"Ken didn't find my clothes in your bedroom or see me kissing another man in my office,'' she said in a defensive rush. ''And I didn't recognize a dress from some little liason with an ex-lover and smile at the memory . . . and I didn't bring an ex-lover in his apartment and make love to him while Ken waited to tell me some very important news and I'd been waiting two whole nights to . . . to t . . . tell yoo . . . ou," she cried, burying her face in the hollow of his neck.

"Kelly, Kelly . . ." Mac chided, his angered manner disarmed by her tears as he stroked her hair with his hand. "I'll go through this one time, because I think you're worth saving," he told her gently.

Kelly pulled her head away in anguished confusion. "You . . . you mean you don't want a di . . . di . . ."

Mac put his finger to her lips to silence her. "We'll discuss that in a moment," he assured her, one corner of his mouth tilting slightly as he handed her his handkerchief.

"Now, about Monica. The key word you used is *ex*-lover. I will not be accountable for anything I did before we were married," he warned. "As for my jacket being in her room, Richard and I moved out to the patio to talk, away from the cleaning crew, and she joined us. I gave her my jacket when she complained of being cold and I guess she wore it to her room after she left her father and I who were still going strong just a little before dawn."

"But . . ."

He pressed her lips into silence again. "I know,

I promised to be right up, but Richard got on one of his soapboxes and I couldn't very well walk out on him. As for my kissing Monica . . . it was she that made the move. Had you stayed, you would have heard me tell her exactly how much I loved you and that she and I were finished, even if it cost the account. Now, about the dress," he went on as he recalled another charge. "I bought that for her birthday, a designer dress I think she called it. We were to go the club to meet Richard for supper. He was delayed on the golf course, so we rode out on a cart to meet him. We all got caught in a cloudburst, Richard with a stalled cart, and ate with green club tablecloths wrapped around our soaked clothing. It was a memorable occasion," he reflected with a degree of sarcasm. "More humorous now than then."

A distorted giggle erupted against his chest as Kelly pictured the three of them sitting in the country club setting wrapped in tablecloths. One by one, her husband had lifted the weights of her desolation off her heart. How easily Monica had maneuvered her, playing on her insecurity.

"And you jumped to conclusions on the stock, too, love," he continued, cupping her chin to watch the spark of happiness catch in her eyes. "Kelly, look around you and then go look in a mirror," he advised her wryly. "I don't need your stock and I married you because I fell head over heels in love with you, you reckless, crazy dummy."

Her freed heart leaped for joy at his last words. And he had been jealous of Ken, something reminded her. "Speaking of jumping to conclusions, you were a little jealous of what you thought you saw in the yard between Ken and I."

Again the corner of his mouth twitched. "It showed, did it?" he admitted with the resigned question. "Well, I didn't know what to think. But . . ." he said, pinching the end of her nose, "Instead of going berserk, I asked Mr. Hudson myself what was wrong with you and it all fell into place when he answered that Monica was up to her usual tricks. That's why I wanted to talk to you."

Kelly could feel the color of her shame flooding her face. Mac was completely right. She had acted foolishly. She had let her emotions run away with her. With lowered lashes, she admitted her folly, tagging on a shaky apology that was accepted with a kiss.

"I will let you get away with it this time," he told her mischievously as his hand slid around her waist to rest on her stomach, "because you had a reason to act irrational. I understand it's a common symptom. When I found out you were expecting, I nearly went crazy."

"Oh, Mac!" Kelly laughed, catching his face in her hands. "I love you, crazy or not!" She planted a loud kiss on his lips that were spread in a full smile when she drew back.

"Now, about the divorce," he reminded her,

forcing the upturned corners of his mouth back down. "I'll give you six weeks. At the end of those six weeks, if you still want a divorce, on my word of honor, you shall have it," he quoted, his last words whispered against her neck.

The series of tingling kisses that ran up the side of her neck to her ear deliciously diverted her attention from the hands that unzipped her dress. They slid the straps off, lowering the bodice to her waist to give him a tempting view of breasts, now anxious for his deliberate seduction. Warmth rushed through her veins like wildfire, fanning her desire for him.

It was like their first time on the beach as they lay on their discarded clothes, exalting in the rapture of the moment. Through the fevered sensations that bombarded Kelly's brain as Mac commanded response from the body he had tutored in love, a singular thought managed to surface. It would not take six weeks to know that she wanted to spend the rest of her life with this man.